17.95

The Moralist of the Alphabet Streets

The Moralist of the Alphabet Streets

a novel by Fabienne Marsh

Algonquin
Books
of
Chapel
Hill
1991

Published by

Algonquin Books of Chapel Hill

Post Office Box 2225

Chapel Hill, North Carolina 27515-2225

a division of

Workman Publishing Company, Inc.

708 Broadway

New York, New York 10003

Printed in the United States of America.

Library of Congress Cataloging-in-Publication Data

Marsh, Fabienne.

The moralist of the alphabet streets : a novel / by Fabienne Marsh.

p. cm.

ISBN 0-945575-47-5 : $15.95

I. Title

PS3563.A7144M67 1991

813'.54—dc20 90-48576 CIP

10 9 8 7 6 5 4 3 2 1

First Printing

For Richard B. Sewall

Socrates: *I maintain, my friends, that every one of us should seek out the best teacher whom he can find, first for ourselves, who are greatly in need of one, and then for the youth.*

—*Plato,* Laches

Contents

Part One: The Alphabet Streets

Part Two: Geography of a Soul

Part Three: The Dunes of Provincetown

The Moralist of the Alphabet Streets

Part One

The Alphabet Streets

On my volcano grows the Grass
A meditative spot—
An acre for a Bird to choose
Would be the General thought

How red the Fire rocks below
How insecure the sod
Did I disclose
Would populate with awe my solitude.

—Emily Dickinson

1.

The Neighborhood and Custer V. Daniels

July in Mainsfield brought so many storms that grown men and women were counting *mississippis* between the flashes of lightning and the cracks of thunder. It was buggier than ever and there were more tiger lilies, more black-eyed Susans, and, after the rain, battalions of slugs and deeper bouquets of air. Everything alive seemed to assert itself, especially in our pond. Rude sounds filled our backyard with a chorus of croaks and belches, and one species of frog sang in diphthongs, much like a Jew's harp.

This morning the front of our house is just as boisterous. Trumpet vines on our front porch are shaking with conversation. Last night my best friend's stepfather suggested Custer consider the sanitary toilet seat business and that is the subject at hand. Mr. Welsh told Custer that, with all the communicable diseases out there, *a revolution in sanitation* is brewing and the financial opportunities are astounding. Never mind the fact that, for the rest of his life, Custer will have to own up to making plastic slipcovers for toilet seats that molt before your very eyes every time you press the button next to the flusher. Never mind that he will have to find less embarrassing words to explain what he does for a living in the same way men who sell brassieres say they are in the foundation business.

I am disgusted.

I know I have a tendency to dwell on things—my family and Custer have told me so—but this toilet seat venture has triggered my larger concerns about the neighborhood this summer. What worries me is that Mr. Welsh's idea is just one symptom of the general upheaval and madness I see around me—one which takes no prisoners and affects my own family as well.

My grandmother Grace thinks Mr. Welsh's plan is a good one. She has seen Mr. Welsh on television and thinks that because he is handsome and enjoys a large, faithful viewing audience he is also brilliant.

I know better. And I do not like to see Custer pricking up his ears because he likes Grace and sometimes listens to what she says in the dire way soldiers hear parting words before going off to war. If Grace is keen on Mark Welsh's toilet seat venture it might influence Custer at a time he is looking for guidance. Instead of wasting his brains on other people's rear ends, Custer should go to college. And if Mr. Welsh is too cheap to send him then Grace should pop for it. She's loaded.

The mention of sanitation has once again set Grace off on one of her favorite subjects: life in microbe-ridden countries.

Today she picked Argentina. She urged Custer to think of *the international opportunities in sanitation*. Any country remotely close to the equator will benefit from individually sanitized toilet seats, she said. She pointed to Argentina as the country where microbes have infested the brains of the population at large. Why else would Evita Perón's body have been stolen several times? Why else would some grave robber have sawed off Juan Perón's hands? And why else would Perón, when he was alive, have demoted the country's most famous writer from head of the national libraries to a chicken inspector?

That's enough.

I am sympathetic to my grandmother's curiosity about faraway places. Doubly so because the only time I left Connecticut was to visit New York City (an hour and a half away); once to visit Maria, and many times to be treated for my illness. So when Grace gave me W. H. Hudson's book on Patagonia, I felt she understood the part of me that wants to escape.

When Grace finished talking, my eyes met hers with a porcelain stare: I would like to return to a serious discussion of Custer's future because it is my belief that Custer and I should make something of our lives. But even Custer is more interested in my grandmother's ramblings. Grace has recently been reading the Before You Go medical section of our *South American Travel Book*, which tells you that bats are likely to bite your toes at night, and supplementing the information with a supermarket biography of Juan Perón. The result is that she knows many things about bats, amoebas, vinchucas; and she grafts this knowledge onto her sensational understanding of Argentine history.

To divert their attention, I told Grace and Custer to look at the sugar maple in front of us. When this was greeted with silence, I pointed to our magnolia, whose cupped-white blossoms dipped in the color of wine promised the coolest, firmest bits of life in an otherwise oppressively humid day.

"Got anything in there on Grenada?" Custer asked.

Yesterday, Custer found out that his real father died in 1983, when the President sent troops to rescue medical students in Grenada.

"Did you find out for sure that your father was on the mission?" Grace asked.

"No."

"Well then, how can you be sure he's dead?" I asked. Custer rarely talks about his father, so I renewed my interest in the conversation.

"Oh he's dead all right. My grandmother told me. First he was telegram dead. Now he's cemetery dead. I just don't know the details."

"Well this won't help you." Grace had found the page. "It was written before Prime Minister Bishop was assassinated. Spice Island. That's all it says. Lots of nutmeg. Just like the President said, 'It's not just nutmeg that's at stake in the Caribbean—it's America's national security.' Remember that?"

"I remember the ground kisser," I said.

"Let me look up nutmeg for the heck of it," Grace said. "Which ground kisser?" she asked as an afterthought. Her reading glasses slid down her nose the instant she bent her head to look at the index.

"One of the medical students. He got off the plane at some U.S. Air Force base, fell to his knees, and kissed the runway."

"Here we go," Grace interrupted. Her glasses fell on the book. With a quick yank, she seized them—then poked them back on. "Tree sap from the nutmeg family is used both as hallucinogenic snuff and as a cure for fungal infections of the skin." She looked up. "Meredith, honey, remember the medicine you took that came from the Madagascar periwinkle?"

Of course I remembered.

"How big is the island?" Custer asked. He was not cutting me off. He knows I hate the way Grace hops from one subject to another with staggeringly insensitive ease. When she skipped to a map of the Windward chain and pointed out its southernmost island, Custer looked as if he had swallowed pink chicken, or something equally troubling to his system. His father's military career had always been a source of great pride, but when Custer saw Grenada on the map, he cried out, "You call that an island! Looks like a gnat left his mess on the page. I coulda taken that sucker with a slingshot!"

Custer was a Southerner, an accented one when he got worked up. He said he did not want to think that his father had died defending a speck in the ocean. I referred to some famous specks in history, which, however small, had played vital roles in the hearts and minds of men, but Custer was unnerved. He changed the subject.

"Show me where it says that stuff about magnolia leaves and nutmeg—You're makin' it up!"

"Says it right here," Grace said. "Besides, there are a lot of things I know if people bothered to ask." She snapped shut the pink plastic bar that had freed itself from a row of foam curlers set tightly on her head and started dabbing her armpits with a Kleenex. "A lot of people don't find time to talk to senior citizens. They think we're not interesting." She closed her book, then folded her pink robe over her matching nightgown and took off her glasses in order to better meet Custer's gaze.

I think Grace has a crush on Custer, and I have to admire any woman in her eighties who has the energy and presence of mind to bat her eyelashes like a true coquette and smile demurely with teeth that are her own. Grace looked fresh, despite the heat, impeccable, despite her night's sleep. Above all she looked confident that she had won Custer's attention and sympathy.

We took Grace in because she is lonely. She has outlived her two husbands, though she had no intention of doing so. My sister Lenore says Grace will outlast us all. Already she is eighty-six and if anything her obsessions—intellectual and personal—make her hang on tighter. For example, this is what she says about her sister.

"I hate Marietta with all my heart. She'll be the death of me! My red hair's made her jealous of me from the day I was born."

"But nowadays your hair is white as chalk," I said.

"You're missing the point," she said. "Marietta looks at my hair and she sees red."

"How old is Marietta?"

"Ninety-two."

Let sleeping dogs lie is what I say. I have red hair, yet Lenore, Maria, and I get along perfectly well. Lenore is thirty-two; Maria is twenty-eight; and the ten-year gap that makes me eighteen and one-quarter has to do with the fact that I replaced a little boy who died.

I myself stayed back a year in school to be treated for leukemia. But they have found the cure.

We are all together this summer whether we want to be or not. Before my parents left for Europe, I worried that adding Grace, Lenore and her children, plus Maria to the household would put pressure on a family that has already been destabilized by my father's recent retirement.

Right now, Lenore is the tense one. Her marriage is on the rocks and she temporarily thinks men are worthless, especially the ones who are after Maria.

I use my work to keep my lid on. I am reading Word Power books in preparation for college entrance exams. This has resulted in my fairly large vocabulary which I detonate on a selective basis.

Custer tells me that I am smart and very pretty, but this has not stopped him from sniffing out a seventeen-year-old classmate of ours (Custer and I are eighteen—I stayed back for reasons of health; he repeated a year when he moved into our neighborhood and changed school systems) who wears a great deal of eye makeup and whose pneumatic figure renews its legend daily.

I have recently met a new boy in our school who is handsome and brilliant but, unlike Custer, derives his intelligence from a great deal of hard work. This Sunday I have invited Jonathan to our family Scrabble tournament, both to consider him as a boyfriend and to test his vocabulary. I do not understand how words like incubus and succubus will increase my chances of getting into a good school. But since I feel somewhat deserted by Custer, for reasons I will explain, it is just as well I have words to help me pass the time.

As if Custer did not have enough problems, I think he has fallen in love. His moods have been swinging to the pendulum of his girlfriend's whims. I have seen this happen before, only much worse, when my sister Maria fell in love during her fourth year of college. Maria, who is by far the sweetest and most passionate of us three, turned into a real stinker. She was miserable, defensive, and a dangerous person to be around. "I hope *you* fall in love," she would say, "then *you* will understand what I am going through."

I had just turned twelve at the time and was not in love. I tried to understand why she was storming off by herself on windy evenings. Then I tripped over a cache of English novels by her bed and instantly knew what had polluted her mind. To break the spell the Brontë sisters had cast on her, I polished off *Wuthering Heights* in two days; then I confronted Maria.

We do not have "fens" or "moors" in Mainsfield, I told her. Only curbs and blocks organized by the alphabet—Annadale, Benningdale, Clayton, Doverdale, Evandale, and so on.

We live on Highland, which is a little different because we are lucky enough to face the last working farm in Mainsfield. Potatoes were a cash crop after the British founded our town in 1732, but since then the land has been chewed up so often to build houses that if the British could see the landscape now they might not feel so bad about having lost the war.

The first housing boom in our neighborhood provided homes for families like ours, with parents who lived through the Second World War or Korea, and whose sons had draft numbers for Vietnam. The second wave—which, thankfully, has not affected our town as much as others—absorbed and is still absorbing a newer crop of young people, who have never experienced war, and who, even after the stock market crash of 1988, owned more cars and things by the age of thirty than my parents accumulated in an entire lifetime.

I honestly do not know what happened to the generation in between. The only representative of that age group is Mr. Welsh, who is forty-six. During the Vietnam war, he dug sanitation ditches in Thailand.

Our Alphabet Streets have an unusual assortment of families—one black, one Hispanic, one Japanese (only for two years), one French, one Italian, and two Jewish. The rest look as if they have just gotten off the boat from England. Our family's lineage is so impure that every time I sit down to get the family tree out of Grace, I run into another severed branch. "So what if she never married?" Grace always says. "Bastards in those days were a lot more common."

Finally I just gave up.

The farm opposite our house was once part of a larger estate called Thompkins Manor. In 1982 the land was bought by a young couple who got rich drawing unicorns on greeting cards. They changed the name to Hydroponics because water, "giver of life," they say, is crucial to their farming method. Their lettuce is raised on mineral water and is grown in a greenhouse, so that when it arrives at our local supermarket it has long roots with no dirt attached. From my perspective, since I do not mind a little dirt, the best thing about the farm is the unobstructed view it offers of a cornfield.

Maybe this last bit of expanse was responsible for unleashing Heathcliff in the moors of Maria's imagination. But still, I told her, "in Mainsfield we don't have men like that." We have boys like Custer V. Daniels, who know less than I do about love, but who, either out of good-naturedness or a sense of entrapment, seem willing to go along with their girlfriend's commitment to the sentiment.

The "V" in Custer's name stands for Vietnam. Do not ask me to explain why George and Louisa Daniels did this. Even Custer thinks it is odd. He knows her father's middle name was Verdun, so there seems to be some consistency to the naming process: pick a military debacle, conceive a son to assign the name to, and there you have it—a middle name appropriate for the times but awkward for the person destined to carry it.

Every time Custer asks his mother why she chose Vietnam as his middle name she either says, "George wanted it" or "V's ran in the family." Since Mr. Daniels was strapped with a lest-we-forget middle name, perhaps he thought his son should have one, too. Builds character, some might say. What is more, military names were in the air near Fort Bragg, where Custer grew up. Custer was told that Troop B of the United States Airborne, in which George V. Daniels was once an officer, traces its lineage to General Custer's command and is called to action with a horn! And finally, I have noticed that when V's or any other naming trend catches on, it sticks with a family like a bad chromosome.

This is no excuse.

Custer's mother rarely talks about her first marriage. She met Custer's father in Fayetteville, North Carolina, but they were originally from neighboring towns in Mississippi. If there was a funeral for George Daniels in either Aiken or Pine Grove, Custer says he did not hear about it. And in 1982, Louisa Fourchette Daniels married Mark Welsh, whom she had met one year earlier at a ballet benefit.

The marriage brought Custer up north, where he started junior high in our school system. Neither Custer nor Louisa saw George Daniels after the legal separation in 1981, when Custer was ten years old.

All I remember from October of 1983 are the television reports of marines being pulled out of the rubble of the United States Embassy in Beirut. A few days later, the President was talking about troops in Grenada, saying, "We got there just in time." Shortly afterwards, I came down with leukemia and was too sick to help Custer sort things out.

Custer has always been private about investigating his past, as if pursuing answers might leave him more vulnerable than a son wants to be with his mother. "Ask too many questions and they know too much about you," Custer says. He reasons that mothers find vulnerabilities the way spiders find eyes. In the middle of the night, just when you are open to the darkness, when a misplaced sock can take on the shape of a gun, that's when spiders and mothers operate, hovering like succubusses.

To his way of thinking girlfriends are just as problematic. Before I got sick, Custer wanted me to be his girlfriend. I was only thirteen and I said no thank you. I think he wanted me to be his girlfriend because he missed his father. Also because I am not like his mother and am definitely not like his girlfriends.

"I like a woman who don't take my shit," he said.

And since I do not take his, and since he thinks I do not take anybody's, his conclusion, the logic escaped me, was that I would make a model girlfriend.

But I don't think Custer has ever had a model girlfriend. The only woman he ever told his middle name to, and therefore the only woman he has ever really loved, also does not take any crap from him. In fact she downright abuses him: The day Custer confessed his middle name to Carmencita is the day she blabbered it out to our eleventh grade history class and started calling him Saigon.

To be fair, Carmencita is from another culture, and does not understand the painful memories the Vietnam War holds for our country. But even so, she can be callous. After our history teacher showed us the TV footage of a Buddhist priest setting himself on fire in a Saigon street, Custer threw up. And for two weeks he would not pick up Carmencita in his beat-up Thunderbird because it meant purchasing gasoline; at the time he was having trouble distinguishing between gasoline as a motor fuel and gasoline as a vehicle for human protest and sacrifice.

Carmencita had no such tension. All she knew was that she was reduced to taking the school bus every day. She wanted to keep Custer as a boyfriend, but if he did not shape up she would find another suitor, certainly one who owned a car.

During that period, Carmencita started bumming rides from Mr. Welsh, whose hired car passes the Alfonso house daily. I told Custer not to put up with Carmencita.

"You're taking crap from her," I said.

Custer told me it was none of my business, and assured me that he understood women. "Besides," he added, "there are compelling though not obvious reasons for putting up with her." He must have meant sex.

From then on I called her Sex.

Not to her face.

My mother and father are in Paris on their second honeymoon, and it is just as well. My father's retirement has broken our hearts.

After he retired my father dressed up anyway. Every morning he would put on a suit and tie, walk down the stairs that led to his office in the basement, and wait for a client to ring. Everything about him was in a state of readiness—the personal computer his company had given him on his last day, the new business phone, the new pencil sharpener, the new coffee pot. He had purchased these items in a spirit of optimism that no one who loved him dared question.

When the phone rang, we would not pick it up—even if the call came in on the regular line. Everybody waited for father to say "I've got it!" More often than not, we would hear him say "Honey, it's for you," if it was for my mother; or "Red! It's for you," if it was for me.

My father and Custer sometimes call me Red, but my real name is Meredith. Actually my hair is glossy chestnut and I have no freckles, except for seven of them on my left cheekbone, which my father calls the Pleiades.

Fortunately, it was not long before my father's business picked up. And by that time he would have been fine anyway: He had discovered painting, and, especially, the nude. He carried home canvas after canvas of every nude who had modeled for the life drawing and painting class he was taking in nearby Essex. His fellow classmates, who were mostly friends of my mother, worked on landscapes or still lifes with what father called "callous disregard" for the naked professional at the front of the class.

When male models showed up, the women in the class were more likely to paint. According to my father, you could measure their generosity with a ruler: I heard him tell my mother that her friends exaggerated mens' private parts to the point of distortion.

My father painted the male models, but they did not inspire him. All the male canvases came back as portraits—"passport photos," Custer called them. The end result is that our basement, where my father's paintings cover every inch of available wall space, is filled with fleshy women and bodyless men. Since he took his easel with him to Europe, I am expecting the same female-male ratio of European bodies to heads when he returns.

"Every Salomé has her John the Baptist," he says.

Mother insists that people come in through the front door.

Our street is quite ordinary, and we have a modest house on it, which has been stretched to a bursting point with all of us home this summer. My favorite part is the porch facing the Hydroponic cornfield—offering, from either side, the best views of our neighbors' houses on Highland Road. Behind our house is a pond with wood frogs that blow up their throats like bubble gum, and beyond that is the playground of the elementary school my sisters Lenore and Maria attended.

Custer's parents live at the end of Highland Road in a house that looks like a small castle. It is a rich person's house because it is mostly vertical. The majority of the houses on the Alphabet Streets are horizontal.

Before this summer Mr. Welsh rarely yelled at Custer. He saves his best yelling voice for the business speeches he gives. But these days the slightest provocation seems to trigger Mr. Welsh. On two occasions, the fights were so bad they managed to rile up their own dog, Rufus-Coco, and a host of other dogs in our neighborhood. Lafayette, a white labrador belonging to Mrs. Pederson, is particularly sensitive to arguments in the Welsh household. When Custer escapes out his back door and storms through our pachysandras, Lafayette is always by his side.

Mrs. Pederson knows what is going on because she lives next to the Welsh's castle and has seen Custer dart through her hedges, widening the hole Lafayette has been working on since she (*Madame* de Lafayette) was a puppy. Mrs. Pederson acts like a toughie, telling Custer he will have to mow her lawn for free, but really she is a warm-hearted Frenchwoman who sings foreign songs as she cleans, and who raises her children in a European manner. This means that her daughter Colette has to come straight home from school and study. It also means that Mrs. Pederson's son Justin is not allowed to play football, "that barbaric sport!" with my nephew, Patrick, whom we call Monstro.

I have never liked Custer's parents so it is just as well they live farthest away. Louisa Welsh thinks she is an artist because Balanchine once remembered her name when she was a *soubrette*. Mark Welsh is a famous pontificator on business issues. His vocation grew out of fifteen years' experience consulting; his work involved walking into steel conglomerates, textile mills, and electronics companies, looking around for a few days, and telling men like my father, who have spent their entire career with one company, that such-and-such a division had to go to make the company more competitive. Then Mr. Welsh would leave it to men like my father to decide exactly who had to be fired. When the bloody work was done, senior managers would step in to ax men like my father, and get the company, as they often put it, on the road to recovery.

Six years ago, Mr. Welsh turned forty and decided he wanted to be taken seriously. He wrote a best-selling book, opened up his own consulting company, and started giving lots of speeches, some of which can now be purchased on audio cassettes at airports. He is much too fat for television, but, because he has a handsome face and a great deal of energy, cable channels have given him a Sunday morning show opposite the religious programming. Before Grace knew who he was, she called him "the sweaty evangelist on Channel 50." Now that he has inscribed her copy of his best-seller ("To my Immortal Grace") she finds him charming and takes what he says as Gospel, including his stupid advice about Custer's future.

I would not harp so much on the Welshes if Custer were not involved. I think Custer has been feeling smaller about himself as the Welshes' house has gotten bigger. His parents recently started turning their garage into a living space for Custer when he comes home. But Custer is not gone yet. Mrs. Welsh's changes have delayed its completion. She insisted on running the plywood beams from north to south, even though they had already been installed from east to west. At no time did anyone bother to ask if the final result would reveal this twenty-thousand-dollar subtlety. Mr. Welsh deferred to his wife's judgment, and, while construction is taking place in Custer's old room, which is being converted into Mrs. Welsh's new dance studio, Custer sleeps in the tower of the castle.

Now that I see what is happening to Custer and his family I find it reassuring to watch the morning talk shows. My conclusion is that there are lots of sick people in this world and that relatively few of them live on our block. Today's edition of *Let's Face It!* had three obsessive-compulsives on it. The first one would come home from work and clean until three o'clock in the morning. She would take a break for dinner by eating the sandwich her husband prepared for her, but she would only eat it over the sink, while she was washing the sink.

Some men put up with a lot.

The second woman worried about germs. Not in the way Grace thinks of microbes in Argentina. Oh no. This is worse.

Woman #2 has clipping files on the bubonic plague and more contemporary subjects like herpes and AIDS. She washes her hands every few minutes—and I never got to the third woman because I turned the second one off when she said that her boyfriend was supportive of the fact that every day she washed her hands until they bled.

From the kitchen I could hear that Grace had turned *Let's Face It!* back on to hear what the third lady had to say. I chose instead to discuss the program with my sisters over tuna fish sandwiches and, in Lenore's case, pepperoni. Maria said that Mother and Father had been right to restrict our television watching when we were growing up. Lenore said that I should not worry about the obsessive-compulsives. "They'll probably start on the lecture circuit tomorrow," she said, "and the following day somebody'll buy the movie rights. They'll make more money in a week than Dad has in a lifetime!"

Lenore is very smart. So what if she is not pretty? She got stuck with the ugly name, too, even though it has beautiful origins. My parents honeymooned in Paris, and conceived Lenore after a dinner at Le Nôtre. The following day they left the city on a night train from the Gare du Nord. Since they had tried twice, to make certain they would get her, they combined the sounds of both locations, not knowing which one they should credit.

2.

New York City and How I Got Maria a Boyfriend

My illness taught me something about time. First, I learned what it really means to live each moment as if it were your last: You live with a sense of the ending even when your cancer is in remission—not in a sad way, but in the same simple way that makes you credit the sunset for a purple you might otherwise have ignored.

I also learned not to pussyfoot around if there is a job to be done. Not until last summer's visit to New York City did I realize just how much this way of thinking had become a part of my life.

And in the spirit of this new frankness, which I know can border on self-righteousness, as Custer sometimes reminds me, I found myself asking Maria what was so great about New York City.

Last August I visited Maria in New York. I have seen people with legs black from street filth except for the pink parts which are either sores or open scabs. They sit on the steps under Maria's window, and one of them shouts out the same thing every day, several times a day, God knows how many times a year: "HEY! Listen—*you!*" He will address a pedestrian or the concrete sidewalk in the same accusing voice.

"Cat got yer tongue? *Fuck you!* Sunny side of the street?!"

Then there is the matter of street noise. Herds of trucks from the Midtown Tunnel thundered by Maria's apartment, then turned the block and came to a stop at the light, brakes screeching like elephants. A few hours later, garbage trucks jarred us out of our sleep—with a *clunk* as they received the garbage, then an ear-splitting grinding noise which was too loud to incorporate into our dreams. The next morning we awoke to wailing sounds. The street was deserted except for a young man crawling on his knees in the rain as if he were making a pilgrimage. His head was thrown back and his mouth open like a PEZ dispenser.

Maria called 911. And when the police car arrived, a policeman jumped out, ran over to the man, and said something we could not hear. We saw the man stand up. We saw the police car drive away. And we saw the man get back on his knees, throw his head back to catch raindrops, and make his way through puddles with oil slick rainbows on top of them and crack vials underneath.

The following evening a man stood stark naked in front of Maria's building. Again we called 911. This time the dispatcher asked if it was an emergency.

We said no.

We were asked if the man was dangerous.

We said we did not think so.

We were asked if the man was armed.

Maria paused for a moment, then lost her patience.

"Listen," she said. "All I know is that some lunatic is standing stark naked in front of my building. I am sure he has deep psychological problems, I am sure he was not loved, I am sure his father was an alcoholic, I am sure his mother threw him into foster homes when he was a boy, I am sure his wife threw him out of the house, I am sure his children spit on him when they see him, I am sure he has been in and out of jail for selling cocaine and I will bet he has been in and out of state institutions! But you know what? . . ."

I could hear the dispatcher say WHAT? from where I was sitting on the opposite side of the room.

"I DON'T CARE! Get him out of here!"

I did not recognize my sister. Was this the woman who volunteered twice a week in the soup kitchen at St. Xavier's?

Only the cockroaches are suited for city life. And according to exterminator specialists, cockroaches are taking over the city. In the subway I saw Black Flag statistics documenting potential growth rate as four hundred thousand per year:

> *una cucaracha en su apartamento . . .*
> *puede producir 400,000 descendientes en un año.*

One of Maria's neighbors complained of mice, but was reassured by a new trap they have developed which glues the rodent's four paws to a foodless sheet and *guarantees* death by starvation.

These are all the things people like Mr. Welsh do not have to deal with. They breeze into town, check into a fancy hotel, and tell themselves they work harder and better than people like Maria, so they deserve what they get.

But at the time Maria was working very hard. In fact, she had two jobs: During the day she worked as a sound engineer for a television news program; at night and on

Saturdays she was a waitress at Aristotle's Diner.

I was at Aristotle's the day she met her boyfriend Leo.

Leo Malcolm lived on Twenty-third Street, around the block from Aristotle's Diner. On weekends he would stop in for a cup of coffee, then make his way to Fiftieth and Park, where the offices of Thomas & Morris, a consulting firm, were located.

Leo was from Kansas, with a face as white as an aspirin tablet and with short hair that resembled a cut-back wheat field. In Oklahoma, South Dakota, Ohio, and Kansas, a young woman might find Leo the handsomest man she had ever laid eyes on. His eyes were either grey or china blue, depending on the light; and when Leo smiled his eyes never seemed to move —they just hung like marbles.

I have seen some of the dark young men who have broken Maria's heart, so I was rooting for a blond. Leo seemed solid, like Custer; only he was a Midwestern version. This meant that Maria would have to look past his penny loafers (a woman should not judge a man by his shoes), and forget about the touch of stiffness I later concluded came from his German-Episcopalian side. It did not seem a life-stunting trait; to the casual observer it just looked as if whoever made him had run out of elastic.

Instead of focusing on Leo Malcolm's appearance, which, by any standards east of the Mississippi, was never going to set a woman's heart on fire, I thought Maria should judge the man by his regular habits—his weekly devotion to Aristotle's Diner, for example.

The day Leo and Maria met began like most of her days. Her regular customers, the brothers Seymour and Stanley

Kapinsky, waited for their orders: fresh fruit for Seymour, who was dieting, and a tuna melt for Stanley. Maria handed Seymour the matzoh he always used to push the fruit around, upsetting the short order chef's attempt to impose sedimentary order on layers of cantaloupe, pineapple, plums, and cherries.

Leo was watching Maria. He found her funny, kind, briskly efficient; and her delicate, angular features—he confided to us later—seemed beautiful to him.

Every time Maria picked up or placed an order Leo's eyes followed her ruffled apron as dutifully as if he were taking an eye test.

Finally she stopped right in front of him.

"What can I get you?"

Leo had not even looked at the menu.

"Is there something you recommend?"

"If it's a snack you want, try the apple strudel!" Stanley shouted between bits of his tuna melt. "You won't regret it."

"With a little cream on top!" Seymour added.

"All our pies are fresh." Maria said. She told Stanley and Seymour to be quiet and let the man choose for himself.

Leo took a quick look at the rotating pastry display and asked about the lemon meringue pie.

"Constantine makes it himself. It's very meringuey if you like meringue."

"I love meringue."

Leo was staring at a cross-section of the pie, which looked like a lemon rope tow with a white intermediate slope on top. What he really liked, as he also told us later, was to play keyboard in the band he had started in business school. He also liked to ski. Leo was imagining himself skiing with Maria, down the chiffon moguls, toward the earth's crusty rim.

When he came to, he remembered how flat Kansas had been and how much he hated lemon meringue pie.

While Maria was reaching for a pie plate, Leo stared at the rotating pastry display—the cheesecake with blueberries big as strawberries on top, the cheesecake with strawberries big as plums on top, the plums that were now prunes, the baked apples big as grapefruit, the rice pudding with cinnamon sprinkled on it, the pecan pie with pecans big as walnuts on it, the carrot cake with a decorative carrot iced-on. And on the counter, as if to compete with the enormity of each confection behind glass, there were muffins big as popovers, as well as slices of pound cake swaddled in plastic wrap and stacked like bricks.

Months later, in a rare letter to Maria, Leo issued a memo on Thomas & Morris stationery. The subject: Aristotle's Pastry Display. He said it had taken him years to formulate.

> I have been looking for the kind of woman I could share the absurdity of pastry displays with and not feel the weight of their empty ridiculousness. It's not weight really, though, is it? It's volume—chiffon towers and chocolate castles and mounds of cake. And why is it that people can laugh these things off in the same way the tackiness of Los Angeles is funny to some of my clients. And why does it have the opposite effect of depressing me, unless you are around to coax me out of my moods?

So it came as some surprise to Leo when, for the first time in his life, he enjoyed every mouthful of the lemon meringue pie, imbued, as he claimed it was, with the hope of getting to know Maria, of playing his piano with Maria, the hope of skiing with Maria, though he did not know if she skied, though he had no time to ski—working, as he did, an average of seventy hours a week.

Still, he thought of ways to prolong his visit.

"More coffee?"

"Yes—do you ski?"

"Excuse me?"

Maria took an order from an amorous couple who stopped their breathy smooching enough to pronounce "grilled cheese." Leo quickly turned to Stanley to ask for advice.

"I'm stuck on Maria."

"What's your name?"

"Leo."

"Hi, Leo. Say, Seymour? This nice young man is named Leo. He's stuck on Maria."

Maria had returned to pour Leo's coffee. She slipped an extra slice of the lemon meringue pie next to Leo's coffee cup. "On me," she said. "I'll tell Constantine you like it."

Leo thanked her and Maria spun on her heel to claim the grilled cheese for the couple, who by this time were joined at the mouth.

"Stanley, when I said I was *stuck*, I meant . . ."

"I know what you meant. You think I don't know what stuck means! I'm an educated man—went to Stuyvesant High School around the corner, got a scholarship to study geophysics at Cornell, *and you think I don't know what stuck means?* Now listen to me—Maria's a smart girl. She does this on the side. She's got a good job. Something in the music business. Do you have a good job or are you a bum?"

"I'm a consultant . . ."

"A *consultant?*" Stanley turned to his brother. "Seymour, this gentleman Leo is a consultant."

"What's that?"

"People ask him for advice. Like a rabbi. Only he makes more money." Stanley turned to Leo. "Let me give you some advice, Mr. Consultant." When Maria was safely out of range, he commanded in a throaty whisper—"*Ask her out!*"

Leo looked terrified. The thought had occurred to him, but had snuffed itself out as quickly as it had sparked. Later on he would tell us why, and would walk us through every corridor of his then troubled mind. The next few months were killers: weekends were out; weekdays were even worse; lunches were impossible—the next two months of his weekly planner were booked solid with work or with social appointments stemming from work. It would not always be so. One day he would get out of consulting. Six years was enough. One day he said he would make time for the things that mattered: music, women, and, eventually, a home life.

But right then skiing with Maria seemed as remote as the cherry on top of the Black Forest cake in the pastry display. I waited for Leo to make up his mind. The cherry seemed to recede as objects do when tired eyes stare at them too long under a fluorescent light; until, finally, the cherry shrank to the size of its pit, then to a peppercorn, and was about to disappear altogether when, suddenly, Leo turned to Stanley and asked, "How?"

"How what?"

"How do I ask her out?"

Jesus Christ, I thought.

Maria returned to pour Leo another cup of coffee, and Stanley nudged him as Maria slid the check across the formica counter.

Leo looked down at the check and stared so long at the brown and white counter that I was convinced the counter was worthy of Leo's fascination. I looked down too, and stared so long and hard that the browns and whites began to resemble a plastified mink pelt.

"You might want to stop by the men's room before you leave," Maria said.

Leo looked up. "Excuse me?"

"I said you might want to stop by the men's room on your way out—"

Stanley and Seymour had put their silverware down and were hanging on Maria's every word.

"How come?" Leo asked.

"You've got crud on your mouth."

Maria's unblinking candor, tempered by a smile of concern, caught Leo off guard.

"Jesus, Maria!" Seymour muttered.

Maria handed Leo a napkin and burst into giggles. She excused herself and ran into the kitchen, where we could hear renewed explosions of laughter, starting and stopping like a bad muffler.

Out of frustration, I felt like taking her to the nearest garage to get that shaking fixed, or, better still, to remove the part altogether.

When she had recovered, she marched out of the kitchen, walked over to Leo, stared straight at him, and whispered with terrific intensity, "I honestly did not mean to offend you. I thought you might want to know. . . I would want to know . . . what I mean to say is that . . . if I had meringue on my mouth . . . I would want someone to tell me before I went out on the street to face the world . . . I mean . . . what if you had a job interview or something?"

"I understand," Leo said politely. "Will you excuse me for a moment while I do as you suggested?"

I was worried that she had blown it. Maria's sense of humor, which she cannot control, has often proved too mischievous for public consumption. She is either very shy or her boldness, like her laughter, combusts out of nowhere. Whereas Lenore will come on strong to protect her warm heart; whereas Grace will open her mouth and let everything pour out unfiltered; whereas I do not open my mouth enough; Maria will pop, fizz, then brood about being misinterpreted.

Seymour and Stanley had witnessed this behavior once before and, though they were old enough to appreciate her spirit, they understood how a young man who did not know Maria might not. Their concern over Maria's behavior came in a confused chorus of exclamations.

"These days a woman doesn't know how to hook a fella and a fella doesn't know how to ask a woman out!"

"The tsars had the right idea—arrange the whole thing. *These kids don't know the first thing about romance!*"

Maria was losing her spirit. I watched her buoyant mood sink fast as the scoop of vanilla in the ice cream soda Stanley had ordered under stress. Her shyness had settled in. She told Seymour and Stanley she had wanted to help the man out, but agreed that her remark might have been too personal. Suddenly she felt like crying, not so much for that moment, but for all the moments it represented—the moments she wished she could take back.

When Leo returned, Maria immediately said, "I apologize."

"How do I look?" Leo asked, dismissing her concern. He was smiling, and had combed his hair.

"Even better," Maria said to herself—really examining, for the first time, the man from Kansas.

"Good. Shall I pay you, or go to the register?"

"I'll take it."

Leo followed Maria to the register, where Constantine usually sat, and noticed that the shoelaces on her sneakers had hearts on them.

"Like those shoelaces," he said.

After Leo walked out the door, Stanley starting singing his favorite Judy Garland tune with all the feeling his fat little body could muster—

> The moon is bitter.
> The stars have lost their glitter.
> And all because of
> The man who got A-WAY!

I ran after Leo and demanded his telephone number.

3.
Sundays and Mark Welsh

No sooner am I done with one sister than I worry about the next.

I feel sorry for Lenore. At night I hear her wake up.

I can hear her walk down the stairs into the the kitchen. She will not use the upstairs bathroom to wash her face because she does not want to wake us. Under the kitchen faucet, she flushes her face with cold water, then puts the teakettle on the front burner and makes herself a cup of Red Rose, which she carries to the porch.

For hours she will stare at the moon, which is bright as a new coin after the rains have washed it. And when the wind unsettles the trees, a liquid light, much like mercury, spills over each vexed leaf.

I would prefer to see Lenore happy. My brother-in-law John was a good man, but he drank too much. He would hide bottles of vodka in the basement and drink out of water glasses to disguise it. Lenore could not smell the liquor on his breath, which is why John chose vodka. But what Lenore could not smell she began to see—it was John's moods which gave him away.

Elizabeth and Monstro could not understand why one moment their father would be hugging them and the next he would be slamming doors, starting up the car, and shouting "You little shits!" as he drove away. They knew their father loved them, but his moods would have them laughing one moment and crying the next. At least that is what Lenore thought, because John's behavior affected her in the same way.

I get very sad when I think about all this. No one saw it happen. No one knew about my brother-in-law's drinking. And when Lenore got married she was convinced it was for life. Even the priest said that he had never seen two people more in love. When the "Do you take this man" part of the service came up, Lenore did not say "I do." She said "Ab-so-*lute*-ly."

Lenore had no idea that John's family history was pickled in alcohol. She says that when you come from a family where there is no history of alcohol abuse, you do not know what to look for and are not even suspicious. It took her five years to identify the problem, two years to acknowledge it, and another three to leave her husband.

Before giving up, I know she tried everything. She would hide his liquor in trunks filled with woolies. She diluted his wine with grape juice or water. She bought smaller wine glasses. She tried to shame him by sending Elizabeth and Monstro to pick him up in his favorite bar. Then Lenore started going to Al-Anon and they told her to stop all this: There is nothing you can do for your husband if he is not confronting the problem, they said.

Lenore still goes to Al-Anon. It makes her feel better because, just when she thinks something is unutterably private, someone will stun the group with a crazier story—like the one about toothpicks. One woman's husband replaced his addiction to alcohol with an obsession for toothpicks. He would buy box after box of wooden toothpicks, trying each one, until he found the perfect toothpick, one that wedged properly—not too snugly, not too loosely—between his teeth. After poking it between his teeth and around his gums for about fifteen minutes, he would render the toothpick soggy and tasteless (they *had* to be spearmint toothpicks) and would begin his search once again.

Lenore's husband was less successful in his search for substitutes. For a while it was cigars, until he started inhaling them; for three months it was Valium, until he started eating them; then he just gave up—and without telling Lenore he would sneak out to a bar on the interstate called The Venetian Lounge. He would be at the YMCA, he said; but instead he returned soused, not from swimming half a mile, but from his own drowning addiction.

The few times Lenore confronted her husband he swore on his mother's head he had been to the YMCA. Since Lenore was still unsophisticated in detecting the signs of alcoholism, she would say "Let me smell your breath." And my brother-in-law would go "Huh," breathing out; "Huh" in her face—as if Listerine would vindicate him.

Adults amaze me.

Lenore knows she has made the right decision, but when all is said and done, the fact remains that she loves her husband and thinks about him these summer nights. Right now she is turning a letter over in her hands as if she is wondering whether to send it. We have no more regular stationery, so Lenore has hastily scribbled her husband's address on an airmail envelope.

When I look into a darker envelope in the sky, the stars

blink back; their pricks of light strain to let a brain through, some pulsing intelligence that might explain everything if the openings were bigger. Lenore will sit and watch all this until the birds sing, and until the the bar of sky above the cornfield opposite our house turns the color of lava. Gradually the orange blaze cools down to the color of topaz; and finally only the frank blue of Lenore's airmail envelope matches the daylight.

The morning suddenly bore the unmistakable feel of eight o'clock. A welcome breeze ruffled our peonies and the leaves on Lenore's begonia, newly sprung, looked varnished. The Pedersons' sprinkler was fanning periwinkle hydrangeas, which had already been drenched by several nights of rain. As the sunlight filtered through the branches of our sugar maple, 8:00 A.M. announced itself upstairs on Grace's clock radio, and I saw Dr. Pederson leave for work. When Grace came down the staircase after her morning bath, she began chattering the instant she saw Lenore. My sister watched Grace approach the wicker chair opposite her own and ripped up the envelope she had addressed to her husband.

Grace was completely unaware of the mood which had preceded her and entered the morning assuming she was its chief protagonist.

"I don't know about you, Lenore," Grace began, "but I had this dream that Harold who I take care of in the hospital where I do my volunteer work—you know, the one who was going to die, the one who is always half-naked with everything sticking out. Well, he died on me when I was changing his bedclothes. I used to talk to him in the operating room, quote stock prices to distract him if the market was up. I did the best I could. I do not speak Yiddish. I tried to explain what the doctor was saying. Well, he died on me. I think he did. Maybe it was only a dream. I knew Harold when he was a little boy. We were in fifth grade together. He gave me my first kiss. Funny how you remember your first kiss. We had Mrs. Kendall. That's right, Mrs. Kendall. She was our English teacher. He was a very bright boy. I'll never forget Mrs. Kendall. She was beautiful and I was a slave to beauty. Now don't forget I was a very pretty little girl!—prettier than my sister Marietta. I had red hair and ruddy checks. I looked like Meredith—that's not right. She looks like *me*. I would bring Mrs. Kendall the *Tribune* every morning, or offer to clap the erasers . . ."

Maria came down the stairs, praying that the children, whom she had exhausted with swimming lessons the day before, would give her and Lenore an extra hour's quiet. As she approached the porch, she heard Grace's jabbering.

"Harold told me I should go into sales. I said I didn't know anything about sales. But the manager of the dry goods store asked me what I could do. I was only fifteen but I said '*I can sell!*' If a customer wants blue, I can sell her black; if she wants green, I can sell her red . . ."

Lenore said good morning to Maria, then interrupted Grace.

"Grace?" she said. "Grace?"

"Yes? . . . Oh, good morning, Maria . . ."

Maria bent down to kiss Grace's forehead—missed—and landed on a pink scalp line between rows of white hair tightly rolled in curlers.

"I was just telling Lenore . . ."

"Grace?"

"Yes, Lenore?"

"You've *got* to stop talking."

Now Lenore was the only one who could get Grace to do it, but Grace did in fact stop talking. I thought she would pop. Instead, a miniature miracle took place. It was almost as if the pores of the universe had opened up, and we had exchanged our dulled senses for new ones: We could smell the sun heating up the morning; we could see the quiver on the squirrel's tail; we could feel the air on the porch move from one side to the other as Mrs. Welsh's car drove by; we could taste icy whiteness of the peonies; and we could hear the water in our pond stuttering with life.

At least I could.

From where I was sitting in the stairwell, I could see everything, though nothing and no one could see me. I was deciding whether—after an evening worrying about Lenore—I would have enough strength to help Maria with her Sunday job.

On Independence Day, Maria accepted one day's work at our local television station as a sound engineer, and it has turned into a free-lance job. WFUW had called Maria a few hours before "air" because their free-lance soundman had never recorded "live."

In the background Maria could hear the host of the show saying in a slow, tense voice, "Let's get a *pro* in here, shall we?"

The production manager told Maria he had "a disaster" on his hands. He tried the flattery routine—telling Maria that her New York reputation preceded her—and *might* she honor Channel 50 by bringing her expertise to a local station?

Maria explained that she was based in New York and that

she was taking a few months off to develop her own sound system, which would involve patented equipment. She was easing out of sound work for television, she said.

Fine, fine, the production manager said, but could Maria help them out with their new business show. Just this once?

I have never known Maria to turn down anyone in need. She asked if she could bring an assistant sound technician. When they gave her the okay, Maria turned to me and said, "Let's go."

When Mark Welsh walked into the studio I thought my jaw would stay unfastened for the rest of its working life.

It took Mr. Welsh a full ten minutes before he realized that the woman with dark brown hair, whose soft curls were neatly pulled back with combs, was my sister. For starters, he had no idea she was a working person. Also, he was busy memorizing his script. Maria's style was so unobtrusive—it was only after she had run a wire from his waist, through his jacket, and had pinned the microphone under his collar, that she looked up and spoke to him.

"Okay, Mr. Welsh," she said quietly. "You're all set."

I heard all this on the headphones and looked up from the oscilloscope. Normally at this point I would say "Sound level fine. Sound ready!" That is what Maria has trained me to say when I am checking her audio levels. When she says, "Speed," it means that everyone has to shut up because she and the cameraman are ready.

But never mind that stuff. What I was doing this time was registering Mr. Welsh's shock and pleasure as he recognized Maria. I know this man and he cannot fool me. He looked extremely controlled, but I saw something go mushy inside him when he looked at Maria. Mr. Welsh smiled an iceberg-melting smile I have never seen. And to my horror I watched and heard him being funny, smart, and—goddamn him—charming with my sister.

"See this script," he said very softly, pointing to water splotches I could just make out from ten yards away, "Your nephew's cannonballs are responsible."

What was he talking about?

Then I remembered that Mr. Welsh had been sitting in a lounge chair working on his manuscript last week, on the day Custer had let us all come over for a swim.

Mr. Welsh's eyes were shy and appealing; but above all, they were reading destiny in Maria's large brown eyes. He was begging Maria to remember his presence that day.

Maria smiled.

Then Mr. Welsh smiled that Titanic-sinking smile again.

I have not talked about Maria's professional side, the work which, until last year, Maria had to supplement with waitressing jobs.

We have been told that she is now one of the best sound-people in the business. You would think that someone who was both shy and bubbly would be incapable of unifying her personality for a serious job, but this is not so.

My sister takes me with her because she wants me to learn about the business. So I know what a Nagra recorder is as well as what mixers, lavalieres, and wireless systems do. If I hang around these people long enough, I can fake their language. But I cannot fake Maria's ear for sound.

And I have no technical ability whatsoever.

This said, Maria refuses to give up on me. On Sunday she let me listen with the headphones and watch the oscilloscope while she was rehearsing Mr. Welsh. I could hear him say, "Fellow Americans, October 19th—Black Monday—was a love tap! *You ain't seen nothin' yet!*" I turned down the volume because Mr. Welsh is a screamer. "What this country needs in the 1990s . . ." He turned toward the studio audience that had begun to appear, "What this country needs, ladies and gentlemen, are *first rate products!* As it stands, they *suck!* Nobody wants them!"

Danny Dorino, the production manager, scampered out of the control room and pulled Mark Welsh aside. "Suck" is as strong as you can get on cable television. Then he stepped over the writhing black cables attached to our studio cameras, and made his way over to Maria and me. "Listen, I should warn you guys," Mr. Dorino said, "this guy's a little temperamental. He's soft-spoken off the set, but when he gets going, he's a nutcase."

Mr. Welsh's performance was brilliant. When viewers called in, he smiled, told them what an excellent question they had posed, and proceeded to address all sorts of issues—budget deficits, stock market crashes, Europe in 1992, interest rates, foreign competition, and Hong Kong's return to Communist China in 1998—as they affected the average person. "I'm glad you asked that," he would say, or, "My son is looking at colleges, so I understand your concerns about saving up for your daughter's education."

No subject was safe from Mr. Welsh's analysis. Superconductivity, the pharmaceutical boom we could expect with biotech drugs, and supercomputers as they related to the transformation of the workplace. *"We're talking about change!"* he would shout, "we've all been digging our heads in the sand through a period in history as significant as the Industrial Revolution!"

When he quieted down long enough to answer more questions (the switchboards were jammed), Mr. Welsh's voice became reassuring. He sounded so funny and so compassionate that I began to wonder whether this was the same man who sometimes yelled at Custer. Maybe the hygiene business was not such a bad idea. When a member of the studio audience asked which industries offered opportunities for entrepreneurs, Mr. Welsh's advice was at least consistent with what he had told Custer.

"Crazy as it sounds, I believe an opportunity exists in the nineties—and right up through the year 2000—to capitalize on people's paranoia. I'm no expert on infectious diseases, but you don't have to be Louis Pasteur to appreciate a phenomenon that has revolutionized our thinking about everything from sex to death. Look at the numbers involved! Everything from syringes to biotech pharmaceuticals to prophylactics to toilet seat slipcovers presents us not only with socially responsible work in public health, but with big buck opportunities as well!"

The minute the show ended, before we had a chance to remove his microphone, a cable television executive who had seen the show called to ask Mr. Welsh if he would be interested in signing on with TV-World. By satellite *The Mark Welsh Business Hour* could be seen in dozens of countries, including the United States. Mr. Welsh eagerly agreed to discuss the offer with Maxwell Firestone, the chairman of TV-World, and, after hanging up the phone, he exclaimed to Danny Dorino, "Let's keep this crew on for the duration of the show!"

Maria was polite, considerate, and professional—just doing her job. I reminded myself of the thirteen billion times in her life Maria had been thoughtful or considerate. What about the time she had hooked up a tape deck, an amplifier, and speakers in my hospital room—complete with remote control! Thanks to Maria I had listened to the Bruce Springsteen tapes Custer bought me, as well as to the Edith Piaf songs Mrs. Pederson had sent. Maria is always thinking of other people—buying Leo less conservative shirts, babysitting for Elizabeth and Monstro to give Lenore a break, taking books out of my hands and dragging me outside to ride bicycles with her. If there is anything she can do to make anyone's life easier, happier, or more amusing, Maria will do it.

So why is it that fear came over me with a slow tweeze between the ribs when I saw the intense expression on Mr. Welsh's face and the smiles Maria returned in his direction?

Danny Dorino approached my sister. "I know what you said about your own business, but you might want to think about Mark's offer. It's only one day a week—Sunday. And we'll do the best we can to match any previous salary."

Maria pulled off her headset and was about to respond when Mr. Welsh, who had finished shaking hands (rather vigorously) with the cameraman, made his way over to us.

"Nice work, fellas," he said. Maria shook Mr. Welsh's hand and thanked him. My eyes avoided his handsome face and were focused somewhere between his neck and his shoes, on the widest part of him.

Underneath all that blubber is a very smart man. A man

who knows that I am Custer's best friend. He knows he cannot win me over easily because I know too much. He knows that up until one minute ago I thought his career choices for Custer were insane because I told him so. He knows I think his wife, who thinks she is an artist, is nothing more than a vain woman with too much time and money. He knows that the more he uses vignettes in the show about the escalating costs of his wife's converted garage or the college his son (on-air he says son; in real life he says stepson) is currently seeking, the more I think his fat ego is running for president.

He knows all this and more.

So why did Mr. Welsh reach over, rough up my hair slightly, and say, "Nice goin', Ace"?

And why are there times in life when there is so much confusion and muck inside, you do not know whether to warm up to someone for the kindness they seem to be paying you, or to punch them in the face for the villainy they have demonstrated toward the people you love?

Then I wondered if I could blame it all on Mr. Welsh. After all, it was Custer's mother who had married the man; it was she who had ceased to defend Custer—probably because she was so desperate to remarry everything took second place. And to be fair, there was also the possibility that Custer's mother honestly saw Custer's welfare linked to her securing a husband.

I don't know. But deep down I think I have very little respect for this kind of desperation. But then again I have not been there. And in the mail when we get those plastic trinkets from Indians saying you should not judge a man unless you have walked a mile in his moccasins I think of Mrs. Welsh.

Still. Eighty-five percent of me believes in passing judgment.

And 98 percent of me does not approve of Mr. and Mrs. Welsh. Yet all of me approves of Custer.

When I get into these moods about right and wrong, Lenore tells me to stop thinking so much (she always knows exactly where she stands). Grace always offers her opinion of the person I am assessing (which always confirms my suspicion that she is an atrocious judge of character). Maria is sensitive enough to appreciate what I am wrestling with. And Custer calls me The Moralist.

4.

Scrabble

(Little Acts of War)

Scrabble is often played in our family when we are trying to foster goodwill, restore order, or award a title; but like many forums set up for diplomacy—my history teacher's description of the United Nations comes to mind—"its goals are often subverted by its signatories," or, in the case of this evening's Scrabble game, by an old member contesting a new member's rights.

Tonight's new member was Jonathan Black. I had invited him to increase my Word Power, as well as to destabilize Custer, whose happiness in love was beginning to get on my nerves.

Already an argument had started over the scorekeeper. "He can't add!" Custer said when Lenore, as a welcoming gesture, appointed Jonathan the scorekeeper.

"Shut up and pick your letters," Lenore said. Elizabeth and Monstro were in bed and she had no patience for anything short of adult behavior.

"Jonathan can't add and anybody who took trigonometry last year *knows* he can't add!"

"Shut up and pick your letters," I chimed in. I turned to Jonathan and apologized for Custer, making it clear that we would be allies during the course of the game. "Don't be so competitive," I snapped to Custer. "It's only a game."

"I don't want to play," Grace said. She shoved her letters toward Custer until the rack hit his arm. She looked at her favorite friend of mine with extreme disappointment. "If you cannot play a polite game of Scrabble then I don't want to play."

"It's not you I've got problems with, Grace, it's this . . ."

"I don't care *who* it is. Behave yourself!"

Jonathan was ahead of the game. He had lined up his seven letters and was shuffling the wood squares as quickly as his mind was dictating words.

"I've got a B; I start," I said.

There was nothing the matter with my first word, BERRY, though by Custer's reaction you would have thought I was illiterate. "What a dumb-ass word," he said.

"How many points?" I wanted to know. Ten points was not so dumb, especially since the first player gets to double the score. And twenty points is definitely not dumb.

Custer went to the refrigerator for a beer. By the time he returned, it was his turn. Maria had plunked SCAB on the board, covering a Triple Letter Score for a total of fourteen points. Custer tucked his flannel shirt into his jeans, as he always does when he is buying time. He does it unconsciously, and it is very appealing because it gives a female an opportunity to watch his strong hands and follow their quick neat movements over his rugged frame. Custer is built like a soccer player, only better, because the body type maintains itself over a higher altitude of six feet or so. Then Custer caps off the gesture by running his right hand through his straight dark hair, freeing his deep brown eyes from the stubborn fringe that often settles over his right eyebrow. Custer reached for his letters, one by one, muttering "I'm a genius" the whole time, and put down YLANG to make a right angle with my BERRY. Then he started whistling.

All my life I have hated whistlers—good, bad, or mediocre. I hate the way they feign ease when, really, there is not a more uptight kind of person around. "I hate it when you whistle," I hissed. "If you are so relaxed you should sing a few bars." I respect a tone-deaf singer more than a robust whistler.

"Besides, I challenge you!" I shouted, with perhaps more zeal than was called for.

Custer was well into his beer and his reaction, one of surprise, was delayed by the alcohol. When he saw that I was serious, he squinted with disdain, as if to suggest I might even be incapable of reading Bud off the beer can.

"Jonathan, dear, how many points does Custer get for that?" Grace asked, peering over her glasses.

Jonathan looked up from his letters.

"None," I maintained, "I challenged him. He's wrong."

"Eleven," Jonathan said, finally doing his job, but oblivious to my challenge.

"*Eleven!?*" Custer shouted, "That's bullshit! Let me count . . ."

Lenore told Custer to calm down. "Don't be so competitive," she said.

"NO points," I said, this time more forcefully.

"Well, if it's a lousy eleven points then I'm pulling it off. I can do better than that . . ."

"You can't," I said.

"Whadda you mean I can't?"

"You put it down. It's wrong. And I challenged you."

Custer stared at me, trying to read behind my eyes, but I would not let him in.

"Those are the rules," I said, and to provoke him, added, "Don't be so competitive."

"Competitive! *Me!?* I'm playing with a bunch of fucking piranhas . . ."

"Custer!" came Grace's sharp yell.

"Sorry, Grace. I'm playing with a bunch of sharks," he corrected himself, "and you're telling *me* to calm down?"

I now realize that the energy Custer might have expended on Carmencita that night was probably the same energy that was expressing itself through his temper during the course of the Scrabble game. But Custer was either too stupid or too good-hearted to give his anger a focus. He should have been mad at *me*. Because my purpose in having Custer there was not entirely altruistic. While it is true I said no-thank-you to being Custer's girlfriend it is also true that I have wanted him to persist in thinking me desirable—*not* for the reasons that I am sure drew him to me: steadfastness, strength of character, and all of those Girl Scout idiocies that have nothing to do with real life—but for myself as a female person, even if he cannot have me. Part of the reason I invited Jonathan was, yes, to help Custer and me get better SAT scores (a Merit Scholarship is Custer's only hope for college), but also to let Custer know that I am a hot property and to stir up the pot a bit.

When things get too quiet around our house I like to stir up the pot.

And there was nothing the matter with Jonathan, who had light brown hair, light brown eyes; everything about him was light brown, except his alarmingly full lips which were always pursed when he was thinking.

Maria came to Custer's defense. "Oh, come on, Meredith," she urged. She was skipping over my pigheadedness, attributing it to the moment, and appealing to the Meredith she knew, the fair and reasonable one. "Give him a break," she said, "we don't really play like this . . ."

But I was playing for blood.

"YLANG is not a word," I said.

"It's a perfume," Custer said. "I know for a fact it's a perfume." He was trying to control himself. "But I ain't arguin' with a bunch of goddamn ignoramuses over a word I don't even want to keep!" In desperation, he appealed to Jonathan. "Yo, Webster! Wake up! YLANG—it's a perfume isn't it?"

"I believe it is."

For one long second I thought Custer might be right. Jonathan had flipped over to Custer's side, not for reasons of allegiance, but in order to uphold a simple truth.

Just my luck—what if Jonathan and Custer were right? If anything it's a poison, I seemed to remember, or maybe a poisonous tree; but whatever it is, I resolved, it's two words and hyphenated.

"It's YLANG-YLANG," I said.

I was on my own. Jonathan had abandoned me. Lenore was thinking about her husband and keeping track of the number of beers Custer was drinking. Maria did not know what the answer was, but thought I was being unreasonable. And Grace was nursing a six-letter word.

"Look it up," Maria suggested. She passed the *Official Scrab-*

ble Player's Dictionary to Lenore, who was suddenly eager to contribute to Custer's downfall.

"I don't trust you!" Custer shouted, grabbing the book from Lenore.

"Give it to me," Lenore held fast to the dictionary. "And you've had enough to drink!"

"Don't go tellin' me I've had enough to drink! I don't need another mother."

"Everybody hurry up so I can go," Grace said. "I've got a word that'll knock your socks off!"

Custer went into the kitchen to get another beer, came back, and used the condensation on the can to write "Hi!" with his finger on Lenore's side of our glass table. He patted Lenore on the back in an effort to make peace, but that evening she was not responding as she usually did to Custer's conciliatory gestures. She was taking his and all gestures as little acts of war. None of us, including my father, would ever get our revenge in a board room, a conference room, an academic hall, or any other place of social veneration. My father paints, Maria has her sound recording, Lenore has her big mouth, and I have Scrabble.

Lenore was busily looking up Custer's YLANG in the dictionary, saying what a lousy dictionary it was, and that if Custer's word was there it would only prove what a lame-brain dictionary it was.

Grace finally realized there was a substantial dispute over YLANG, and looked up from her letters long enough to admonish Custer for his second beer. "My *third*," he said, toasting Lenore.

I have often wondered how so much poison could drip from

a fangless mouth. But what amazed me even more was how Custer could diffuse bad feelings as quickly as he had generated them. No sooner had he said that to Grace than he got up, walked over to her, and kissed her cheek. He was as sweet as he had been bellicose, until Lenore's findings proved me right.

YLANG-YLANG, in the Scrabble world, and in the real world, a tree, *Canangium odoratum*, from Malaysia, and also a fragrance, very poisonous. But most important: it was two words and hyphenated.

"HA!" I exclaimed. I could not help it. Custer would lose eleven points, forfeit his turn, and, for the rest of the game, possibly scale down his obnoxious behavior.

"Gimme the dictionary!" he said to Lenore.

"HA!" I shouted again, grinning from ear to ear, and slapping the thigh of an alarmed Jonathan.

Lenore slowly, gracefully, demure as the lady Grace had always wanted her to be, said, "Why certainly, Mr. Daniels." She handed Custer the dictionary.

"Piece-of-shit dictionary!"

Maria started to giggle.

"A *fine* one," Lenore said, "the *best*."

Amidst the excitement, Grace slipped AMOEBA on the board, hooking up with Maria's SCAB. "How many points?" she wanted to know.

Jonathan wrote down Grace's score, then he looked at me. My eyes confirmed his nagging fear. Jonathan seemed to understand that his ignorance of *Canangium odoratum* had cost him his one chance to impress me. My mind took a picture of his thoughtful expression—the pursed lips, which now sawed at my nerves, and the brown fuzz above his lip. Suddenly I felt an inexplicable combination of pity and disgust—the way I sometimes feel in elevators when a passenger breaks wind and cannot find anyone around to blame.

Somehow the volatile situation relaxed into a fairly civilized game of Scrabble. I say fairly civilized because there were, of course, the routine squabbles over time allotted per turn, with the accompanying Jeopardy theme song signaling time's up hummed by Maria, co-hummed by me, and at times joined by Custer when it was Lenore's or my turn. Grace rarely hummed. Jonathan did not know how. Shamed to the bone, Jonathan resigned. Without Custer he said he would consistently have botched up the scores. He insisted that Grace take over the scorekeeping and be put in charge of the egg timer as well. "I don't *believe* this," Custer said, rolling his eyes.

The pressure was too much for Grace, though she was too proud to admit it. Maria, through a deft system of hand signals, offered to slip grandmother an A, which Grace did not refuse. While this was going on, Custer was trying to figure out how he could cover Triple Word Score. His heart was not in it. Something had broken his concentration and Custer seemed only marginally interested in the game. I suspected he was thinking of Carmencita. But it was not that. Maybe he was wondering about his father. After any crisis in confidence Custer has this recurring nightmare. He is traveling mile after mile in the Chesapeake Tunnel on his way north. Mr. Welsh is telling him that if he does not shape up he will end up spending his life in the little glass booth deep in the heart of the tunnel. A surge of memories from happier times with his real father wells up. Then he awakes.

But no evidence of that, either. Finally, Custer's brooding glance fixed itself on Jonathan.

Meanwhile, Lenore had recovered her usual feistiness. She had started whistling, conceivably to annoy Custer, but successful only in irritating me. Then she began humming the Jeopardy theme song until Custer exploded.

"I can't concentrate! And you took twice as long!" Under the pressure of all of the players, minus Jonathan, humming along in solidarity, Custer hastily came up with SUFFER.

I suddenly felt Custer looking at me. I glanced up from the board and saw him staring at Jonathan, but his eyes quickly came back to mine, as if to ask me what my feelings were toward Jonathan. A pang I could not decipher jabbed me between the ribs. I shifted my gaze to Grace and watched her jiggle her letters around with hands that for the first time struck me as old; the veins came up like blue garter snakes. And just as I was vowing to myself to be more patient with Grace, Custer called my name.

"Meredith, can I talk to you for a second?"

"Here?"

"No. In the kitchen."

I excused myself and told everybody we would be right back. I had no idea what Custer wanted to discuss, but I was so nervous I knocked my letters on the floor.

"What are you doing?" Custer asked, when we were in the kitchen.

"What do you mean?"

"What are you doing?" he repeated, this time more forcefully.

I did not say anything.

Custer grabbed me by the shoulders and made me look at

him. The light was dim and his pupils became so large and black he frightened me. His face was closer to mine than it ever had been. The thought crossed my mind that he intended to either bite me or kiss me.

"I don't know what you mean," I said.

Custer hid his face in the space between my neck and my hair, resting his chin on my shoulder. He took a deep breath, mumbled, "Red hair smells good," then, embarrassed by his sloppiness, recovered his anger.

"*Stop* messin' with me, Red. You *know* what I mean! This whole setup has nothing to do with Scrabble!"

"You're drunk," I said.

Custer shoved me away, then dropped his hands in remorse.

"I'm *not* drunk—but even if I were I'd still know you were messin' with me!"

"Hurry up!" Lenore shouted from the living room. "Grace is winning!"

"Red?—"

"What?"

"I'm sorry I pushed you away like that. The last thing I want to do is hurt you."

I followed Custer back into the living room and pretended everything was normal.

Grace had managed to cover a Double Letter Score, along with the Triple Word spot Custer had left vacant. The word was PARASITE. "Now, let's see," she said in the quiet, ladylike voice that befits a cheater, "How many points does that make?"

"Now, let's see," Maria echoed. She had allied herself more closely with Grace in our absence. "That's three, four, five, six with the Double Word Score, seven, eight, nine, ten, eleven —eleven times three makes thirty-three!"

"Hold on a minute," Lenore said, "Doesn't Grace get a bonus for getting rid of all her letters?"

Jonathan, our ex-scorekeeper cum legal counsel, trotted out the Scrabble game cover and read Rule #17. The rule would change the course of our game that evening, and the future of all Scrabble games in our family:

> Any player who plays all seven of his tiles in a single turn scores a premium of 50 points in addition to his regular score for the play.

"So wouldn't that make eighty-three points?" Grace asked innocently. And because, when it comes to Scrabble, laughing and cheating go hand in hand, the *most* peculiar, ladylike whimper-laugh overtook Grace's skinny Yankee body. Of course, it was not long before Maria's insides began to rattle, too. I think she would giggle less if she let her laughter go like a good honest sneeze; it's the way she holds back that makes them release *sforzando.*

Under normal circumstances, Rule #17 would have caused Custer to blow up. But he was silent, which alerted everyone that something had happened in the kitchen. Maria stopped giggling. Only Grace was focused on the game. When Custer's turn came, Grace gently reminded him that, according to her egg timer, his time was up.

Nerves of steel, our Grace! Most gentle when she is winning.

"Time out!" Custer cried suddenly. "Time out!" Custer rolled onto his feet, stood tall, then, on second thought, glanced at the players seated on either side of him—Maria and myself

—and instinctively carried his rack of letters into the bathroom. When he came back, Maria and I looked at each other, acknowledging that my friend Custer who drives me crazy was aging well. He was growing into the kind of man you see in the Rockies, wearing blue jeans, a simple flannel shirt, and an honest expression, when he was not being a drunken horse's ass. Which at the moment he was not.

His next word was BETTER.

"Six points," I calculated. Pathetic, I thought.

"A moral victory," he said quietly.

I honestly do not remember who won. But it must have been Grace, followed by Maria, trailed by Lenore. I do recall that Custer, Jonathan, and I were neck and neck for last place.

Then that prairie-howling cat bitch Carmencita called.

5.

Carmencita and Custer's Swimming Pool

The next morning our thermometer hit eighty-nine degrees on the porch and I brought down the fan for Grace. It said Igloo on its square frame, which gave us unrealistic expectations. Seconds after we turned it on, the fan buzzed and scratched more loudly than our crickets in full chorus; its blades moved the same hot air from one side of the porch to the other, which was better than nothing, but which was accomplished at the expense of the day's peacefulness.

I reminded Custer of the swimming date he had arranged last night with Sex. In a way I was testing Custer. I wanted to know if his affection last night had meant anything, and I soon received my answer.

"Gotta go, Grace," Custer said. The mention of his girlfriend stopped conversation as abruptly as a crucifix arrests a vampire. As for me, I felt a stake go through my heart. I admit it—but the good thing is that now I know where I stand and nothing else can hurt me.

"Now listen," Custer suggested to Grace, "Why don't you go upstairs and sit in the air-conditioning for a while?"

"Don't mind me," she said, disappointed that Custer was leaving, "I'll just sit here and rot."

Grace's martyr routine was very well done and, as if to tell her so, Custer reached over to pat Grace on the shoulder.

Elizabeth was upstairs whining about her hair and Monstro was running up and down the stairs to avoid Lenore. Cutting through this fracas, Grace's determined little voice piped up to Custer. "What about that Scrabble game you promised me! Aren't we going to have a rematch?"

Custer promised Grace a rematch and, before he came down, I slipped a comprehensive list of all the two-letter words in the English language into my bag. Just in case.

Elizabeth and Monstro are taking forever. We offered to bring them to Custer's pool so Lenore could have a rest, but Elizabeth is still walking around with a Maxwell House can on her head. Last night she washed her hair, rolled her wet ponytail around the can, and, on her way to bed, insisted that the aluminum tunnel caused her no discomfort as she slept. The desired result is straight hair, and currently she is mad at us because if we rush her it will not work.

"Monstro's not ready either!" she yelled.

And sure enough Lenore and Monstro were in the kitchen arguing about athletic supports. At times like these I bet Lenore is wishing she had not been so wasteful of her husband, no matter how smart she is, no matter how much he drank. We could hear Monstro raising his voice.

"*Custer doesn't wear one!*"

"All men wear them! Don't you want to be a *man?*"

We waited five minutes. The argument showed no sign of resolution. Out of boredom Elizabeth pulled down her Maxwell House can too early; her hair looked like wet kelp, the lasagna kind, freshly cooked. And she was angry.

"You're going swimming anyway," I said.

Custer said he was going into the kitchen to mediate. Before I could stop him from getting involved he had pulled Lenore aside and whispered, "He's right, I *don't*."

I hate the way Carmencita takes her time when we pick her up. We have driven ten blocks out of our way to get her on Evandale when, from where we were, we could easily have walked down the block to Custer's pool.

When we pull into her driveway in Custer's fifteen-year-old Thunderbird, she sticks her hand and *only* her hand out the door, holds up her please-wait index finger; then for eight minutes her house looks like a funeral home, showing no sign of life, until, finally—and sometimes she takes as long as seventeen minutes—she emerges like Miss America taking her final walk, smiling, waving, and walking nice and slow so everyone will look at her for the last time.

Only it's never the last time.

Carmencita is pretty and she knows it. She is tall and thin, and where she is not thin she is not supposed to be. Sometimes Carmencita draws attention to those more substantial areas, but she is always unpredictable. It is as if she wakes up the Catholic daughter of Luis Manega Nelson Alfonso one day, and the next day she wakes up like the woman in the opera she is named after.

I find these two sides very confusing because, though it is none of my business, I cannot figure out if Carmencita and Custer have done it or if she is holding out on him.

Custer is very discreet in these matters. He would never tell me. But I get clues just by watching Carmencita eat and drink. The other day we went out for Mexican food and I saw Carmencita try her first margarita. She did not drink it like the rest of us. She made a whole production out of it, reminding us of her half-Cuban half-Nicaraguan background, and demonstrated the proper way to drink a margarita.

For starters, she removed the ice cubes. A real margarita does not have ice cubes, she said. She drew an arc with her index finger like a deaf person making a letter and scooped up an ice cube, which she slipped in and out of her mouth as quickly as if she were pulling the meat off a stalk of asparagus.

Carmencita's exaggerated gestures were already causing a stir. People from neighboring tables wanted to know who the dark young beauty was. The more aware she became of the attention, the more dramatic her performance got—and when Carmencita finally got around to drinking the margarita, she managed to out-tart the lemon. Her index finger and thumb held the lemon wedge up; and her little finger circled the rim of the glass, collecting salt as it went. "You are supposed to taste the lemon, the salt, and the margarita at the same time," she said. She managed to suck the lemon without making it look like the mouthguards the young men on our football team wear. Then she ripped off the rind, made a bold display of its pulp between her teeth, and hid it in her mouth until she had emptied the contents of her drink. After she had swallowed the whole mess, she spread her legs, lifted up her glass, and shouted, "Done!" as she slammed the glass back on the table —"like a true *caudillo!*"

We tried to keep up with her, but my entire body was tingling after my first; Maria would not stop talking about Leo's upcoming visit after her second; and Custer, because he was our driver, prudently retired after his third.

Carmencita had four. And when she had finished her last one she repeated the name of the drink so many times that *margarita* finally slurred into the only line of poetry her body had ever retained. "*Margarita esta linda,*" she said, "Margarita is beautiful."

She would not stop. Some dead Nicaraguan poet named Rubén Darío was speaking through her, she exclaimed. She commanded us to spread our hands around the dinner candle, pinkies touching.

By this time the eyes of the men at neighboring tables were upon her. Her firm bust had not exactly grown bigger, but it had grown more confident and was positioning itself like a separate person at the table. Her body was acting one way and her face another—so while her anatomy looked ready for the nickname I had given her, Carmencita's face looked pure and detached. Her head was tilted to the side like Joan of Arc's hearing voices. "*Margarita esta linda,*" she said.

The women at the neighboring tables were using words like "disgrace" in a very clipped way. We could hear a quick hiss, followed by the second syllable, *-GRACE!*

In a restaurant filled with confident women Carmencita would not have caused such a commotion. But I could not help thinking that Carmencita's future would be fraught with conflict because, though she considered herself first and foremost a friend of great loyalty to women, women did not trust her. She once told Custer in no uncertain terms that he could never replace her female friends, whom she valued more than any boyfriend. One of the reasons I am so often included in their excursions and dates is that Carmencita likes me. Yet I have never extended my friendship to her.

Custer's response to his girlfriend's quirky solidarity was consistent with how I imagined all men might react: Instead of putting him off, Carmencita's statement had the reverse effect of driving Custer wild, so that he would try to please her in every way. Based on this observation, I have developed a strange picture of Carmencita's future, wherein she will exhaust men with demands they feel compelled to satisfy, though she will never have requested them. Men will be attracted to her, will obey her rules of engagement, and will be more attentive to her than to their girlfriends or their wives. Then, when she has thoroughly exhausted them, they will probably return to their less demanding girlfriends or their more relaxing wives. If at a later date the men are feeling strong enough, they will once again sniff out Carmencita's company in order to reassert their manhood as well as their loyalty.

Carmencita's singular ability to be both wily and honest might even result in her asking the men why they are incapable of sustaining this exemplary behavior in the relationships they already have. And I could see the men (who can be very stupid) being intrigued by her perceptiveness.

This cycle would repeat itself and revolve around the same central irony: Carmencita would attract men, be left by them, and seek the support of her women friends, whom she loved, but who continued to envy her.

I suddenly had a flash of Carmencita living a very lonely life.

On second thought, I am not taking into account Carmencita's tremendous vanity and capacity for survival.

In fact, I must be drunk! There is absolutely no evidence

that this will happen, or that Carmencita is worthy of any sympathy whatsoever.

Custer and Carmencita are playing Marco Polo and they are spending most of their time underwater where a lot of feely-touchy is going on. This makes me mad. If I am not doing it, I do not want anybody else doing it. And when I am not doing it, displays of affection make me violent.

Mr. Welsh is home working on his next best-seller and pretends that he is not looking. But I know he has been correcting the same page since Maria joined us half an hour ago.

I am trying to understand why, even before the Sunday show, Mr. Welsh kept a valve in his heart open for Maria. I know he respects her. At the same time, she is the only one who has never outwardly despised him. And when people do not tell him he is a repulsive human being, he is the type of person who automatically thinks he has a fighting chance to win their approval or affection.

It is such a beautiful day that Mr. Welsh is not imposing himself on it. He is letting people breathe, and allowing his stepson to be himself—though Custer is not behaving altogether naturally. He is overdoing his passion for Carmencita, as if to show his stepfather that he is a man too, that he has someone who cares about him, and that he can make decisions for himself.

Mr. Welsh is helping Carmencita cheat. "He's over by the diving board!" he will shout. Or "NO!—by the steps!" He is also watching Maria teach Elizabeth the crawl, and is probably impressed with the patience she possesses which he himself lacks.

I am sitting on the rim of the pool, dangling my legs in water that spangles around my feet. In my hands I have five pages of two-letter words that Jonathan copied down for me. But nothing seems to matter except what is going on in the pool—Carmencita chasing her Marco; Elizabeth throwing her head back into the water and shaping fantastic hair styles with her long brown hair that comes up slick and folds like taffy.

Jonathan's words do not matter anymore. And Jonathan does not look as fine as Custer in a bathing suit, which is why my eyes drift off the page, preferring the shine of Custer's back as it slips under the blue-and-white beaded rope to my black-and-white rows of two-letter words.

I feel as dirty as Mr. Welsh, pretending that I am working but really guarding a privacy I do not want. In fact, even Mr. Welsh is more honest than I am. For the first time I see him giving in to the rhythm of the day. He is not yelling at Custer, and he is smiling to himself every time Elizabeth throws her wet brown arms around Maria's neck. When Monstro used the flagstones in front of his deck chair as a runway for cannonballs, Mr. Welsh laughed during takeoff, then watched Monstro's sloppy wet prints evaporate under a thirsty sun. Then *splash*—pool water showered his manuscript; and soon after Mr. Welsh rolled into the pool like a great white whale who had surfaced with a cub named Monstro. As I watched, I wondered what it would be like to harpoon Mr. Welsh and boil his blubber away: How many barrels of sperm oil would he fetch?

Monstro squealed with delight as Mr. Welsh balanced him on his head and threw him into the water. Everyone was confused by Mr. Welsh's friendliness. And when Mr. Welsh swam by Maria for the third time, I noticed how his wet hair, his deep grey eyes, and his relaxed if not happy expression made him look much younger than his forty-six years.

I think he might be losing weight.

And I hope he is not falling in love.

6.

A Dream of Life and The Insight That Is Custer's

I will fry in hell I know I will.

My imagination is visiting places it has no place being.

Last night I had a dirty dream, a ridiculous dream. Yesterday's swim might have had something to do with it. On the way home I kept on picturing Custer's wet back.

I went to bed early, between eight-thirty and nine, and started to read under the yellow circle cast by the lamp above my bed. The rain began stitching my window and grew more persistent, bursting the seams of its delicate pattern with running water. A vein of lightning split through the greyness and water poured from the sky—it smashed at our pond like an eggbeater and churned up white water and mist. The air was suddenly garbled with noise and drew closer, like a shawl. When the sky finally blackened, it swallowed my room whole so that I could not see out anymore. My reflection bloomed on the black window pane, and I turned off the light.

After my illness my mother and father worried that I was dreaming too much, day and night, "observing rather than living," I overheard. It is true I often dreamed about having a relapse and never leaving the hospital. But I learned to take one day at a time.

The thought of dying did not scare me. What scared me was the possibility of a relapse, because relapses mean more blood tests, more chemotherapy, and some of the worst medications known to man.

I was thirteen when I started feeling tired and getting fevers. Then one day my parents came to wake me up for school and saw blood on my pillow. Right away they recognized symptoms which they had seen once before with my brother. I was diagnosed as having Acute Lymphocytic Leukemia (ALL) and was immediately put in the hospital. I got so far behind with my schoolwork, I had to repeat the eighth grade. And when I was not sick or in school, I spent most of my time feeling that life had dealt my parents rotten cards. One sick child. One dead.

But I have been in remission ever since. If nothing happens to me this year (four to five years is the safety period), I will be in the clear. In the past twenty years, doctors have been able to treat childhood leukemia. My brother had the worst kind, Acute Myelocytic Leukemia (AML), which is still hard to cure.

I admit that the thought of living in a hospital the rest of my life terrified me. For a long time, I would close my eyes and see the equipment that was supposed to be helping me. I would see my mother's face, as well as my father's, drawn and worried. I remember asking myself why I had survived leukemia and my brother had not.

But last night's dream was about life. Because in real life what had happened was this: We were taking turns reading in English class when "Death, be not proud" came up for Custer.

Our teacher suddenly remembered my illness and realized that Custer was my friend. He saw how difficult it was for Custer to read the sonnet.

"That's fine, Custer," Mr. Nichols had said quietly, "Let's go on to something else."

By that time poor Custer was all choked up and had come to a sputtering finish, remembering how awful I had looked in the hospital, my red hair gone, and how he had worried about me.

In the dream, part of which was set in the same English class, there was nothing about death. I remember a John Donne poem, but it was the one he had written To His Mistress, which had been Mr. Nichols's favorite until Carmencita's parents objected to the license-my-roving-hands stuff and had our books taken away.

If anything, Custer helps *me* understand the sad things. Or maybe he just knows how thoughts overtake me in ways I cannot shake. I will think about someone who means a great deal to me, and a wave of terror comes over me. I ask myself: What if circumstances had never put us together? or What if the person were taken away? Chance at these moments seems a fragile, desperate thing.

So when I start thinking about all the slender likelihoods from which things grow, I feel how possible it is for everything to slip away, and loss creeps over me like a long shadow.

I have felt this way for as long as I can remember. When I was four I started to calculate how old my mother and father would be as I grew older. Then I would ask myself how old we would be when we left each other for good. For every year of my life I have adjusted the intervals. And each time, I reassure myself all these sorrows are far away. But really I am lying, because in the interim the anticipated grief hurts just as much.

Custer helps me with all this and more. He puts his arm around me and says, "Red, when it happens you'll deal with it. And there's no point thinking about it until then."

He has taught me something else.

He has noticed how I do not finish stories in public. In the middle of telling stories I will get shy and dishearten, as if I do not think anyone is interested enough to hear me through.

I told Custer that I cannot tell stories to people who, in the course of telling my story, give me the feeling they do not care.

Custer said, "Well then, you gotta write 'em down if you can't get 'em out by talking."

So that is what I have started to do.

Custer proposed we start a weekly newspaper. He reads all the computer magazines and, when Mr. Welsh is away, sneaks into the den and plays with his stepfather's PC. On this newspaper we have called *The Highland Chronicle*, he is the editor/publisher and I am the writer. Our circulation is already several blocks long and we are working on Carmencita's street.

Sex is in charge of distribution and sales.

When I run out of material for stories, I stop myself from using real life circumstances. The people I am tempted to write about buy *The Chronicle* so I have to be careful. Custer says we must not alienate the subscription base that Carmencita worked so hard to get.

Since Custer is an editor, he does not understand something writers learn early on. Namely that when I make things up, people think they are being depicted; and when I take things from life, people do not recognize themselves.

This might be because people go through their lives knowing very little about themselves, even less about each other —and it generally takes a breach of security for most people to learn *anything*. For example, if I were to write about what I think is brewing in Mr. Welsh's heart, Mrs. Welsh would genuinely enjoy my story and see it as the purest fabrication of my young imagination.

For this week's paper, I finished reporting the events of the neighborhood sooner than expected and had time to write a story. Most of my dirty story is based on my dirty dream.

Right now we are trying to decide whether Grace should keep the books for *The Chronicle*. I am in favor of this, I suggested it, and I am hoping Custer will come 'round. He is not saying anything, but I know Custer was not impressed with Grace's mathematical abilities during our Scrabble game. I also know that Custer would like to give Grace something to do. How else can we shut her up?

"She might not be good with scores, but I can guarantee you she is good with money!" I said.

"She has no former experience."

"Oh yeah? And I suppose Se—I suppose Carmencita does?"

"Carmencita's credentials are *obvious* . . ."

"*Grace's* skills are obvious! She manages money from two husbands who dropped dead on her! Besides, Carmencita doesn't *care* about our paper!"

Custer did what all obtuse people do when they have run the course of their pathetic arguments. He resorted to statistics. He reached into the front pocket of his jeans, said, "Let's look at the numbers," and pulled out a polka-dotted piece of stationery on which the following was written in Carmencita's big loopy handwriting:

Subscriptions in the Alphabet Streets

1. Mrs. Jacqueline Pederson
2. Mr. John Pederson
3. Mrs. Louisa Welsh
4. Mr. Leo Malcolm (out of town—Maria will pay)
5. Mrs. Grace Soybel
6. Mrs. Irene Mason
7. Mr. Seth Mason
8. Mrs. Desiree Ortega Diaz Alfonso
9. Mr. Louis Manega Nelson Alfonso
10. Mami
11. Papi
12. hermana—Luisa
13. hermano—Julio
14. Ms. Lenore Saunders Donaldson
15. Ms. Maria Saunders
16. Jonathan Black
17. Mark Welsh
18. Mark Welsh
19. Mark Welsh
20. Mark Welsh

"*Big deal* if she signed up her whole family and hit your father four times for money!"

"He approves of this, you know . . ."

"Beats toilet seats," I said.

The only advantage stemming from Mr. Welsh's affection for Maria has been his long silence on the subject of business opportunities in sanitation. I have a feeling Maria is responsible for flushing the subject out of his obsessive brain.

"I want Grace to work on it," I said. "An older person will make the newspaper more legitimate."

Custer tucked his shirt into his jeans and sat down. "All right," he said. "Bring Grace down here and let's talk about it."

I found Grace upstairs in the air-conditioning, sitting under her old-fashioned hair dryer. The bonnet was big, grey, shaped and fluted like a half-opened fan. She looked like Marie Antoinette in her best wig.

The long and the short of it is that Grace refused our terms. She will not consent to being a business manager unless she can write a column as well. The column has to be about what strikes her fancy on any given week—health issues, travel, or essays about senior citizens. She has demanded "full artistic freedom."

Custer and I asked for some time to think it over. On my side it meant giving up sole authorship of the paper. I winced at first, then overcame my selfish instincts. Custer was deciding if Grace's material was suitable for our market; and in the meantime Grace decided to draft a sample column on the basis of which we could refuse or accept her services. She had disappeared upstairs, and the next thing we knew she was back on the porch pecking away at her 1942 Smith Corona portable.

I took the opportunity to slip Custer my story; then I started talking very quickly as if apologies were already in order for a story I suspected was lousy, or controversial at best. I told Custer that it was set in 1969, and that my research was based on the leftover information I had not been able to use for my history paper on students in the sixties. I still had the stack of

Life magazines I was supposed to have returned by June 8.

I told Custer I would slug in new names. "Ignore the names I've used," I said. "They were the first ones that came to mind."

At first Custer was delighted I had come up with something so quickly. But when he started reading, all I could hear him say was, "Jesus!" followed by "Jesus Christ!"

Affairs of Highland Road
(*A Story for* The Highland Chronicle)

The walls in Custer's room were covered with aluminum foil, roll after roll of Reynolds Wrap, which blocked the small window facing the fuchsia azalea that blooms every summer.

The Magical Mystery Tour was playing on Custer's record player and on the table next to it there was incense burning and a 7-Up bottle stretched out of shape, twice as long as it should be. There were candles all around the room, reflected by the walls; each one made up of different colors, all uncomplimentary, so that yellow, black, and green wax collected at the base of each one like a geological overflow.

Custer looked back toward the closet and saw his black leather jacket suspended like a sheet of licorice on a wire hanger. A woman emerged from the closet—"Please put it on," he said to the woman. No sooner had the woman zipped the jacket up than Custer playfully tugged at the large ring at the top of the zipper. "I'll let you out," he said, and pulled the zipper along its diagonal course until he was surprised to find that the woman had no clothing underneath. Custer looked to her face for an invitation, then he peeled away the leather jacket and was about to touch her when she jumped—"Someone's coming!" The teacher, she thought, but the only change in the room were the words to the music. The Beatles were singing different lyrics to the tune of *The Magical Mystery Tour*, and the words were not fitting properly—

License my roving hands, and let them go
Before, behind, between, above, below.
O my America! my new-found-land . . .

The woman ran out of the room, refusing all advances. Custer waited for her return but, after a few minutes, he shot out of the room, only to sink, momentarily, into grass that had become marshlike. The mud was sucking him down, and he stood at the door of the bathroom, grasping the knob. He was sinking fast—up to his knees in ooze.

"I'm coming in," he yelled.

Custer forced the door open and the woman jumped out of the bathtub. She was wet, sad, and snarling—and the water changed from clear water to pond water; the faucet poured out goldfish, tadpoles, and scattered the surface with blinking stars.

"You scared me!" she shouted.

Custer snatched a towel off the rack and wrapped her tightly in a big new towel that covered her knees.

"I was worried," he said.

"You didn't dry me properly," she said.

The curls in her dark brown hair were dripping with water and the steam from the bath and the warm rain outside added to her skin a layer of mist.

"Here . . ." She pointed to the part of her towel that covered her upper thigh.

"There!" he said, briskly rubbing an area that looked quite dry to him.

"Here," she said, pointing to the same spot. The woman had opened the towel and was pointing matter-of-factly to her inner thigh.

"I thought I just dried . . ."

Custer caught on and shook his head in disbelief—he was not entirely displeased. Then he followed her lead. Drops of water from the woman's hair splotched on Custer's back as he knelt below her.

"You're too much," Custer said almost inaudibly. "You're really too much." Then on his knees among broken shells and spongy bits of life spraying from the tap he explored *his America*, he said, *his new-found-land* . . .

Custer finished reading. He smiled at me, then looked down at the story. He cleared his throat and said nothing. He cleared his throat again and said nothing.

Nothing will come of nothing, I thought.

Custer cleared his throat a third time and said, "I'm not saying it's not well-written."

His pencil was tapping more slowly now, but Custer's right foot started flexing and unflexing at regular intervals. I looked into Custer's deep brown eyes as if to ask him whether my feelings should be hurt. When I received no answer my eyes dropped down to his right foot and, since he knew the nervous tic was annoying me, he let me fasten his foot with my eyes. Pencils, feet, and mouths were still. And all we could hear was Grace punching her typewriter.

Finally I spoke. "Does that mean it *is* well-written?"

Custer smiled. "You *know* it's well-written, Red."

I was hurt. Now that we had established the story as well-written, it seemed as if there was nothing left to discuss. But there was everything left to discuss. I felt as vulnerable and as sloppy with myself as Custer had on the night of the Scrabble game, when he had softened toward me in the kitchen.

Custer cleared his throat a fourth time and said that, clearly, the man in the story was both a great naturalist and explorer—"a modern-day Balboa," he said. The woman, Custer added, was someone whose telephone number would have to be made available to him. And the narrator, he said, with a smile and a soft spot in his voice, had created "a masterful female fantasy."

Then he brushed my nose with his index finger in a gesture of affection I could not warm up to at that moment.

"John Donne?" he said. "How about that? Leave it to you . . ." Custer's voice broke off. "I'm glad it wasn't—"

He stopped and ran his hand through his hair. His dark brown eyes squinted slightly, bringing his long black lashes closer together.

He would not look at me.

"I'm glad it wasn't the other sonnet," he said.

Custer looked my way for a fraction of a second. And before I could tell him I was okay now, I was not sick, he turned away and left me so abruptly I could barely hear him say, "Gotta go—"

7.

Days of Boredom and Mr. Welsh's Obsession

I have just finished cutting my toenails and am asking myself if there is not more to life than this. Grace is talking to the plants and swears she has just heard Lenore's begonia scream.

"As long as it's not Lenore," I said.

Grace asked how Lenore was getting on. When I said I thought she was having a rough time, Grace said, "She should be over that by now."

I paused to consider Grace's statement. She should be over that by now! In the sweltering heat I tried not to get too worked up, but my gut reaction was to scream with frustration at Grace's lack of depth, her toughness, or both.

"How do you get over something like that, Grace?" I asked with apparent composure. I would not call her grandmother.

"You just get on with it. Get yourself another husband like I did."

There had been Robert. Less than a year after Robert's death there had been Irving. And yesterday Grace had gone to the grocery store for a case of mineral water and come back with our grocer, Mr. Sneff. Would he be her next victim?

"And what kind of person do you think Lenore should marry?" I asked.

"An older man. Somebody like Mr. Welsh . . ."

"He's taken—"

"I know he's married. I said someone *like* him."

"How about Mr. Sneff? He's sixty-nine."

"Nope. He's mine."

"Mrs. Pederson says he's a fortune hunter. *Un vieux gigolo . . .*"

"He's still mine."

"Even with the cigars!"

"You betcha!" Grace was serious. "But Mark Welsh is a better type for Lenore," she continued. "He's got money. He's an intelligent man. She'll have to play her cards right because she's got two children. Now mind you, she's no beauty either, but she's smart, that Lenore, very smart and funny. And I think someone like Mr. Welsh could handle her."

"Then why did he marry Mrs. Welsh? She's as dumb and boring as they come."

"No, she's not. Louisa Welsh is a smart woman—though most men can't be bothered with a woman who has brains. And it's not the man who does the picking. It's the woman. I bet Mrs. Welsh got her bid in pretty early. In Lenore's case, she'll have to compromise or get her priorities straight. When I married my second husband, I married him knowing that if anything happened to him he would provide for me. Lenore's got to start thinking that way. She's not a teenager anymore."

"You're no teenager either. And Mr. Sneff's a grocer. How much money can he have?"

"*I've* got money, sweetheart. At my age I'm looking for companionship."

"Lenore doesn't trust him. She says money's like perfume to

Mr. Sneff. He can't see it, but he sure can sniff it out."

"Well, Lenore's nose could stand a few lessons—that way she wouldn't have to move home."

"It's only temporary—"

"Is it?"

"She can go back to teaching," I said. I did not want to hear any more.

I do not like to raise my voice. And I do not like arguments. Sometimes Grace has a way of bringing people to a roiling boil; then she acts shocked by their reactions, as if there is nothing in the world worth getting so hot and bothered about. What's more, when people make the unfortunate mistake of disagreeing with Grace, she acts as if she has been personally attacked.

If I pursued this conversation any further I knew what would happen. I would get upset and state my case; then Grace would start crying—not because she is especially sensitive, but because she is a great actress. Disagreements often end with Grace dabbing her wet eyes, saying, "You should not talk to your grandmother that way" or "You have no respect." She deflects the content of the discussion, acts wounded, and issues remain unresolved—comfortably so for her, uncomfortably so for others.

Grace is tough as nails. I found this out after her dog Perón died. I remember her sitting on the porch, rocking in her wicker chair, quietly wiping her eyes with Kleenex.

Grace "loved" dogs. She said she had always loved dogs, particularly Perón. I asked what had happened to Perón, and Grace boo-hooed (she actually made that noise, boo-hoo, just like in the old movies).

"He had ticks."

"But dogs don't *die* of ticks," I said. "What else did he have?"

"He had ticks. Jumping all over him—around his eyes, in his ears. Ticks. What was I to do with a dog who had ticks? Nobody wants a dog with ticks. Marietta wouldn't take him. *My own sister wouldn't take him!*—just because he had ticks."

"So what did you do?"

"I put him to sleep (boo-hoo)."

"You what?"

"I put him to sleep."

At that point I got angry with Grace.

"You killed your own dog because he had ticks!"

"Don't yell at me!" Grace said. Then she started crying.

"I'm not yelling at you. I just don't understand how anybody could kill a dog just because he had ticks."

"Don't attack me! I didn't kill him. I had him put to sleep. Don't yell at me! I'm your grandmother and I deserve some respect."

This is the same Grace who always smiles warmly when we are assembled for Scrabble games or whatever, and who often says, "We all get along so well." She will insist on this. "We should be thankful we have a nice family and we all get along so well." "Don't we all get along?" she will ask, or "Aren't we lucky?"

What Grace does not understand, and what there is no point in telling her, is that her notion of getting along is accomplished by the complete suppression of any personality that comes into contact with hers.

Even today, she said, "Meredith, honey. I count my blessings that I have a granddaughter like you. We get along so well."

Yet seven-eighths of me is at war with Grace.

All I can think of is how bored I am. Bored and pent up. Grace is bored, too, despite her tidy little presence. The difference is that I know when I am bored and Grace does not.

My grandmother's presence irritates me. The nasty little ripping sound she makes as she tears coupons out of yesterday's paper; the way she zips and unzips her makeup pouch, snaps her change purse shut, wipes her glasses, sips her cup of coffee, jiggles the ice cubes in her water glass; or even the way she tries *not* to clack her heels as she walks into the kitchen for her second cup of coffee. These sounds carry me to the brink of madness.

I shuffled into the living room and turned on the television.

Today's *Let's Face It!* was about women whose husbands had become women. A special operation, once only available in Morocco, had replaced their love pump with a button. All this was illustrated with graphics as DR. MORRISONI explained the procedure.

For the benefit of the viewing audience, the identities of the transsexuals and their ex-wives were clarified like this:

MAUREEN, formerly PETER
Ex-husband of Anne
PATRICIA, formerly PAT
Ex-husband of ALLISON

I zapped to another channel when the show host asked Patricia, "But what was it *really* like to make love to Allison when you were a man?"

We get too many channels and I cannot figure out which films were originally in black-and-white, and therefore old, or which were originally in English. On one of the movie channels, I am sure I saw Buster Keaton in "Free and Easy," but he was saying, "*Yo también soy de Kansas.*"

Not that I have anything against the Spanish language; but I would like to hear Buster saying he is from Kansas in English first. And I want to see the film in black-and-white the way Buster Keaton made it. Or else how will people be able to identify the original version of anything? If Grace had not been around to set me straight, I would have thought Buster Keaton with his sad eyes was a Spanish movie star in the early technicolor era.

I turned off the television and returned to the porch, where I found Grace dabbing her armpits. I really hate it when she does this. "That's not good hygiene," I blurted out, thinking I would get her to stop by appealing to her interest in the subject. Then I tried to block Grace out by concentrating on the cornfield in front of me. But all I could see were rows of corn that reminded me of the way Grace sets her hair. Then I thought about people like Leo who grew up in flat places—"*Yo también soy de Kansas.*"

I wish I knew more about people who come from flat places. Where we come from, there are hills; and sixty-eight miles away is a city whose verticality could make you mentally ill. I do not know if I ever will be able to live in New York, but I am certain I will never be able to live in a flat place.

People like Leo who succeed in living in flat places must have an imagination which is more vivid than mine. They do not need mountains to give life contours. Or perhaps their eyes are so famished for variety they are content with the sight of an anthill, which—however flat, stark, and barren the landscape and however starved my eyes might be for a mountain —for me will never be anything but an anthill. My thoughts on Kansas were interrupted by the mailman.

The mail is the most exciting event in a bored person's day. Grace pretended she was writing her column when she saw the white jeep with red and blue markings pull up to our mailbox. I could play the same game.

"Want me to get it?"

"That's all right," I said, "I can get it."

"No trouble?"

"No trouble."

"Because I can get it. Probably could use the exercise."

"Not in this heat. Exercise in this heat is no good for anybody."

Then I did something incredibly cruel. "Why don't you give me a few minutes to make a fresh batch of iced tea? Then I'll get the mail."

I made iced tea the long way. I did not use the packet of powdered instant with sugar and lemon already in it. I boiled water, driving the temperature in the kitchen up another five degrees, poured the water over the tea bags, waited for the tea to cool, put ice cubes in it, sliced up some lemon; then I asked Grace if she preferred sweetener to sugar.

"Don't mind me," she said, her voice straining to be cheerful, "I'm still drinking coffee."

All of a sudden I wondered who would drink the tea. I did not want any. But I emerged from the kitchen with an enormous glass of tea with lemon. I did not want Grace to know I had been bullying her about the mail.

What I usually do when I am in one of these bored and

snitty moods is destroy a perfectly good story I have written for *The Highland Chronicle.* This must be my way of punishing Custer, but he is never around to feel it. The one time he gave me editorial advice after I had ruined my own story, he said, "What are you doing, Red? This stinks and you know it!" He warned me that if I did not do better work he would give Grace more columns to write.

"Go ahead," I shouted, "you don't run the good ones anyway!"

I was referring to my story, "Affairs of Highland Road," which Custer had judged "unsuitable" for *The Highland Chronicle.*

I miss Custer. I miss my editor. I miss my coach.

He and Sex are taking a two-day canoe trip and I am sure he is doing all the paddling. I know he would cancel his plans if I got sick.

But I am not sick.

Some people are like that. They are the best friends you could hope for if you are down, if you are going through personal catastrophe. But God forbid you should have a good day.

Life does not grant people personal catastrophes every day. It takes a little girl falling into a well or an earthquake to bring out the best in people. But in between disasters, people are dying of loneliness.

My only problem is that I am so bored I wait for the mail all day. Today it contained the following:

> One postcard of a Roman viaduct from my parents.
>
> One plastic teepee from the Indians with an envelope asking for money.
>
> One L. L. Bean Fall Catalogue.

One donation request from Sponsor a Child, for children with leukemia.

One postcard for Grace. (Marietta is visiting one of three ex-husbands in Coral Gables, Florida.)

Three bills for my mother and father.

One sample of a new soap called Scrub, which Grace immediately appropriated.

One fat envelope filled with coupons and a sample of perfume in a tiny glass vial.

One Courtland County newspaper (our competitor).

Another postcard from my parents (Hotel-Dieu in Beaune).

One love letter addressed to Grace from Mr. Sneff.

Four fat envelopes for Maria. Same handwriting. No return address.

I am a snoop if someone I care about is involved. Privacy is for people you do not love.

So I handed Grace her love note and did not tell her about the letters for Maria. I rolled them into the newspaper and stopped in the kitchen to pick up Grace's magnifying glass. While Grace sat on the front porch reading Marietta's postcard and examining a new batch of coupons (filial hatred and money come before love), I crouched by the pond, held each letter up to the sun, and looked for any clue as to who the mysterious sender was.

Three out of four envelopes were so thick I gave up. Envelope number four, a thinner one, was my only hope. The sender had used a ballpoint and pressed very hard, but the sentences were still difficult to read because they ran over each other: lines from the bottom half of the letter were folded over the opening sentences. After twenty minutes of inspection with Grace's magnifying glass, I was able to make out the mushiest love letter I have ever read:

> My darling Maria,
> You are between the lines I am supposed to be reading,
> and your face appears to me as I should be writing. . . .
> When you walked into my life this summer with those
> crazy wonderful headsets on . . .

I smelled smoke. I looked toward the house, then realized it was the letter which was smoking. The sun had used the magnifying glass for its own purposes. With laserlike precision, it had cut a small brown spot, which was now the size of a cigarette burn. A small flame had started licking off the corner of the envelope and suddenly I heard Grace call out from behind the screen door—

"Meredith, honey. Somebody's trying to deliver something for Maria. Come on out front!"

I threw the letter in the pond before Grace could see it. Lafayette jumped in to retrieve it, but I shouted, "Let it go!" The letter gurgled as my sneaker pushed it to the bottom. My heart was pounding, my right foot was soaking wet, and my sneakers squeaked with knowledge of my wrongdoing.

On the front porch, an Air Express delivery man had two packages for Maria. I signed for them, but was too rattled to look at the return address. Grace did, however. No name, she said. Just a company whose name she did not recognize. I assumed a guilty Leo was sending Maria presents to make up for yet another canceled visit.

I was wrong. And when Grace asked me how I had gotten my sneaker so wet I wanted to tell her it was none of her business.

The truth is that Mr. Welsh is after Maria. Letter after letter arrives for her with no return address, and Mr. Welsh sends packages from out of town by Air Express. Now I know that yesterday's teddy bear from Miami was from the big teddy bear himself. And today it was slippers from Graceland—two fluffy barges which bore Elvis Presley's face on their fronts like miniature plastic Mount Rushmores. Stuffed in the heel of the left slipper was a brown plastic bottle of Love Me Tender hair conditioner.

From every airport Mr. Welsh has been sending Maria a mug with the city's name on it. Though Maria has been very private about all this, it is difficult for us to pretend that we have unlimited kitchen cabinet space. Already Albany, Schenectady, Cincinnati, Detroit, and Kansas City are hanging from the cupboard, threatening my parents' wedding china with their sturdy presence.

I do not recognize this Mr. Welsh. He is the busiest person I know, yet he seems to make all the time in the world for Maria. The phone calls have started too. If I pick up, I can just make out Mr. Welsh's voice through the crackle of a long distance call. He will say he is looking for his son, Custer. I will tell him Custer is at home. He will be silent.

If Maria picks up, he will talk to her directly—not that she ever tells us he is calling, but the conversations are so long it is obvious. I hear Maria trying to limit the conversation to discussions about the business show, but there will be long stretches where Maria says nothing.

One day he called from an airplane and it was not just to talk about the nimbus clouds outside his window. I heard Maria say, *Paris?* Then I heard her say, No. The next day an Air Express envelope arrived containing a plane ticket. Another mysterious phone call. Another no from Maria.

I do not know how she does it. Everybody has a price, and if someone tried to buy me off with Paris, I would have a hard time resisting. Knowing Maria's tendency to be moved by people's smallest gestures, I cannot understand how she is staying so cool. Especially since Mr. Welsh seems to have keyed right in to Maria's sensibility. He sends her digital recordings of her favorite composers and first editions of Victorian novels.

Mr. Welsh has not had much time to investigate Maria's likes and dislikes, but he does have a remarkable talent for drawing portraits of people he is obsessed with by connecting the dots. So if Mr. Welsh asks Maria what kind of music she likes, she might say—"At seventeen I fell in love with Elvis." And when Mr. Welsh travels to Memphis on business, he will make sure to block out five hours at Graceland. He will hire a special guide, take a tour of the mansion, and absorb every detail of Elvis's life with the singular purpose of informing Maria. After he has romanced her with Elvis, Mr. Welsh will flesh out another one of Maria's enthusiasms from a single dot of information.

During the week, Mr. Welsh spends a lot of time traveling, consulting, and giving speeches to people who worship him. I do not see how Mr. Welsh can love them back because no one can love lumps of people in every city in the United States. In fact, when Mr. Welsh gives the same talk, in every city, to the same thunderous approval of each body of inhabitants, he must have two distinct feelings. The first, to feel loved by gobs of people, and the second, to hold those people in contempt for not seeing through him. Day after day, he repeats himself, tires of his own voice, and must wonder why his audiences do not see him for the imposter he is.

But how can they?

Mr. Welsh makes them feel unique. On the business show, I have seen him make an individual caller feel that he has asked the single most important question ever to be asked on television. Even Maxwell Firestone takes him seriously; last week, as an experiment, he broadcast *The Mark Welsh Business Hour* to European audiences—and they loved it.

Besides, the members of his audience cannot see Mr. Welsh's whole life. They cannot see him running after planes, writing columns, books, speeches—all of which say the same thing to many people. They do not see him chartering flights from New York City to his farm in Maine. They do not see him acting as if he were the President of the United States because when he gets up on their podium he acts homespun, as if he had just stepped off a Greyhound bus and had traveled long hours and thousands of miles to be with the good citizens of whatever city his five-year calendar and his forty-thousand-dollar fee have brought him to.

Because Mr. Welsh puts his life and feelings into different compartments, I worry about anyone he decides he loves. Custer is safe because, though I believe he loves Custer in his own sick way, he does not love Custer as a son. When Mr. Welsh decides to love a woman, that's when he devotes himself to passion. He seems to throw his entire being into it. Like in the movie where Buster Keaton throws himself against that cyclone.

I have to wonder about people like this. I have read about successful, respectable public figures who stare at panty displays in Woolworth's or blow their noses in the shower. In Mr. Welsh's case, whatever is stirring under his publicly likable surface seems much more serious.

But I am hardly the one to ask for an unbiased opinion. And I suppose I should credit Maria with her fortitude. Any other woman smothered with one sixteenth as much attention would have given in by now. What worries me is the single-mindedness of Maria's pursuer—who still wears a wedding ring, plain as day, fat as a preacher's.

8.

Tears of a Linebacker and The Kiss

Lenore is down on men. Particularly older men like her husband. Do not even *mention* Mr. Welsh; and she says Leo has a long way to go before she thinks him worthy of Maria.

She still likes Custer, and her new enthusiasm is Jonathan Black because she thinks he is very good to me.

Lenore never asks me what *I* think, but let me say this: It is my firm belief that Elizabeth and Monstro need a father. Elizabeth shows signs of becoming a domineering little skunk. The girls from her summer camp were nice enough to elect her captain of the cheerleading squad, but already she has had a run in with the quarterback of the summer football team, our neighbor Justin Pederson.

Justin takes football very seriously, and I do not blame him. Mrs. Pederson has finally agreed to let him play the "barbaric sport," so while he is scoring points during the game he is also trying to win his mother's approval, despite her complete disdain for the sport. Every time Lenore bumps into Mrs. Pederson in the supermarket, she says, "*Quel idiocie, çe sport!*"

Justin concerns himself with every aspect of the game, which is why the ten-year-old quarterback of the Raging Tots criticized Elizabeth for leading cheers that reflected her complete ignorance of the game. When the Tots had the ball, for example, Elizabeth would scream—"Push 'em back, push 'em back, *WAY* back!" Or when they had taken an eight-point lead, she would bellow—"That's all right! That's okay! We're gonna beat 'em AN-Y-WAY!"

But the worst is what she did at halftime. This morning Coach Borden pulled me aside and said, "Elizabeth's stealing cheers from the other team."

The girls from Glen Ferry sing in harmony and spring into displays of gymnastic excellence—with cartwheels, splits, backhandsprings—and a great deal of spirit:

> We don't mess around—HEY!
> *We don't mess around!*

Elizabeth's little girls have bodies that do not sing or stretch as well; and instead of cultivating their own pathetic capabilities, they perform a cheap imitation of the Glen Ferry routine. For a cartwheel, Elizabeth substitutes a banana step; for a split, she tells her girls to lunge; for a backhandspring, she settles for a back roll. And if the Glen Ferry girls rally the crowd with—

> Nail those boys and push 'em HARD
> Make 'em fight for every yard!

Elizabeth will immediately compose—

> Fight 'em, fight 'em, fight 'em GOOD!
> Push 'em if-you-can-or-COULD!

From my seat in the bleachers, I often follow Elizabeth's tremendous exertions and see very little payoff. It is like being stunned by the immensity of a pig and noticing, with disappointment, that the whole animal finishes itself off with a twisted little pig's tail. Fortunately for the pig, as well as for Elizabeth, someone has granted them entirely unself-conscious natures—which lets them go about their business without asking or being interested in what other people think.

Monstro was kicked off the Raging Tots today because he cries every time he is tackled. Coach Borden pulled me down from the bleachers and waved his arms in exasperation. "Every time Patrick gets tackled he cries," he said, "*and tackling's the job!*" By the end of the game, I was convinced that Elizabeth would make a fine linebacker and Monstro might not make a bad cheerleader. I took Monstro, still sobbing, home to Lenore.

I wish people like Coach Borden would understand that children who get stuck in day camp for the summer have nothing else in their vacation to look forward to. And it is a bad sign when counselors and campers are privately notching days on the calendar, hoping that camp will end.

Coach Borden had a calendar. I saw it this afternoon when, at Mrs. Pederson's suggestion, Lenore and I walked down to his office in order to discuss Monstro's athletic disgrace. Today is July 18th, and for every day since June 25th I saw a big red X blotting out the boxes on what looked like the kind of calendar a university sends its graduates.

"I see you are marking the days," Lenore said.

Coach Borden looked uncomfortable. He took off his baseball hat. His sweaty hair was matted against his scalp, making him look as if he had just been hatched. "I'm sorry about Patrick," he said, "but I think you understand my position. We can't have a linebacker who cries."

"What's it to you?" Lenore held back her rage, "This is not the Rose Bowl. This is a summer camp. This is the high point of the summer for my kids and you're not even giving Patrick a chance to play!"

"I'm not sure Patrick wants to play! He cries every time we put him in the game—"

"He needs a coach! That's all. Why don't you give him a few pointers—or change his position! Does he *have* to be a linebacker? You could make him a goalie—"

"Wrong sport—"

Oh, shut up. You know what she means, I thought.

"Look, Mrs. Donaldson, I don't want to argue with you. Patrick is just not cut out for the game."

"He needs a coach," Lenore said.

He needs a father, I thought. And so does Elizabeth. We had not even discussed Elizabeth's behavior.

Lenore and I got up to leave. Coach Borden saw us to the door, shook our hands, and as we turned to go, he said, "Tell you what—we'll start Patrick on our swim team."

"That's a great idea!" I said.

Lenore's face was sealed. Coach Borden unhinged it when he said, "Patrick swims a fast crawl and he seems to enjoy it." That got a smile.

I watched Lenore tuck a mousy lock of brown hair behind her left ear and decided that if her marriage was on the rocks she would have to start taking care of herself. Lenore's shapely figure had gotten a little porky; her skin was pale and not very clear; her fine hair was limp and shapeless, except for the one curly lock she was constantly sticking behind her ear.

"That sounds like a good idea," Lenore said, "As long as Patrick doesn't mind."

Coach Borden said, "I'll take care of it."

Lenore and I thanked the coach. When I looked back I saw Coach Borden pull the calendar from his wall and dump it in the wastebasket. Lenore was too busy denouncing her husband to notice. "John should have spent more time with Patrick instead of sneaking out to bars."

That night John called to wish us all a happy Fourth of July. Lenore hung up and muttered, "May he rot in hell!" I did not feel like laughing, especially since John had managed to make the call while he was sober. And I did not correct her; you cannot "rot" in hell, you can only roast. But I did do something I had never done: I told Lenore to shut up. "Shut up, Lenore," I said, "enough is enough." Then she started crying, and I felt awful. She started crying because she knows I love her and that I never speak like that—she knows that for me to tell her to shut up means that she is a mess.

I am sure it is just a phase. After all, she thinks Jonathan Black is an exemplary young man. "What about Jonathan?" she is always asking me.

Jonathan Black is not stupid. He got wind of Custer's canoe trip and called me up because he knows my best friend is away. Last night we went for a walk on the long aqueduct behind the cornfield, which was lit up like a yellow ribbon. The stars were out and Jonathan said he could make out the Southern Cross. I told him that according to Grace the Southern Cross could only be seen from the Southern Hemisphere, say, from Argentina. He said I was probably right, and I knew I had crushed him as effectively as when he had been wrong about ylang-ylang during the Scrabble game.

I cannot help it. I know that you are supposed to listen to boys as if their every word is a gold nugget. But I was not in a romantic mood. And while I was grateful to Jonathan for getting me out of the house, I could not help but ask myself the following question: Why is it that the ones you don't want drop like shoes?

I did not want to talk so I started asking questions to keep Jonathan from asking me any. "Can you find the North Star?" Turns out he could. "And what about the signs of the zodiac?" Jonathan pointed to a constellation he thought was Virgo. With each question and response, I felt more and more like a nursery school teacher trying to keep a child busy.

Then he stared up at the sky and asked about my illness, something I have never discussed with Jonathan. "I would rather not talk about that," I said. Jonathan apologized and quickly changed the subject.

"Lenore told me about Patrick and Elizabeth's difficulties in summer camp. Would you like to talk about that?"

"To tell you the truth, Jonathan, I would rather not talk at all."

The sky was filled with stars—so much so that when I breathed deeply I half-expected to take in a chestful of sparkles. I was sorry to be so short-tempered with Jonathan, but if I am not interested in someone I am the kind of young woman who can just as happily walk alone on an aqueduct in the moonlight. Besides, breakups and brutalities are a part of life. Everything suggests that we live in a violent universe, so why pretend that the conduct of human affairs is any different? I learned from a science program that when stars die they give birth to other stars. So if I turn Jonathan into a dead boyfriend, maybe a million other amorous opportunities will come of it.

The problem is that Jonathan, who genuinely wants to be my boyfriend, has no intention of becoming a snuffed-out nova. He has already tried reaching for my hand, but when I sensed his clammy paw coming at me I shot my arm up and quickly found Sagittarius, the archer, the only constellation I could point to with any certainty.

I kept my arm stiff as a bayonet for a very long time, until my muscles collapsed and my arm came crashing down, resuming its rightful place by my left side, where Jonathan's clammy hand was again set like a trap to receive it.

Without trying to seem too obvious (I did not want to discuss the matter with Jonathan; I wanted him to read my deafening signals), I hopped around to Jonathan's left side, pretending I was demonstrating a dance step. With my one good arm I pointed at the Milky Way until that arm too became tired, at which point I folded both arms against my chest and tucked any leftover extremities beneath my armpits.

"I like you Meredith . . ."

Here it comes.

"I cannot help it. I just like you so much."

I wanted to become invisible, or I wished he would disappear. In any case I did not think it necessary for both of us to endure this discussion.

Out of the corner of my eye, I looked for the disgusting fuzz above Jonathan's lip to remind myself of how repulsive I found him, but I noticed the peach hairs were gone. In the moonlight, what looked like grains of sand catching the light was actually stubble from shaving.

The stubble was coming toward me—

"Jonathan!" I exclaimed.

He was so close I was shouting down his nostril.

"Jonathan—listen to me!"

I clapped his shoulders with my palms, held him at arm's length, and stared straight through his pupils down to his soul. "Maybe I am not being *clear* about this. I really do not want to have anything to do with you in the way you want to have something to do with me."

He wriggled out of my grasp, ran on ahead, and smashed an already dead cricket with his foot.

"That's clear," he said. "That's very *clear.*" He was imitating the way I had said clear, and started walking ahead of me, until finally he shouted, *"In fact, you can't get much clearer than that!"* I had never heard him shout before and suddenly it struck me as very funny.

I burst out laughing.

"What's so funny?"

"You're funny. That's what's funny." I could not stop laughing, and I do not think Jonathan had ever seen me laugh as I sometimes do with anybody other than Jonathan. "What you said—HA!—what you said—was very funny, that's all." I laughed a bit more, then settled into a comfortable chuckle.

Jonathan looked puzzled. "So you think I'm funny?"

This set me off again. "HA-HA! Yes! HA—Yes! I mean sometimes . . . Yes!" I stopped to get my breath. "*Definitely.*"

"Good," he said.

Jonathan thought for a moment and I knew that his brain, after suffering a mild rejection followed by a good-natured reparation of feelings, would return to its usual brilliant working order. No hard feelings. I was also confident that I had gotten my message across, and that Jonathan would never again try to—

"Jonathan!—"

He kissed me and at first I did not respond.

I was shocked by an audacity I did not know Jonathan possessed. I felt his raspy face deliberately rub against one cheek, then the other, as if to say I will try not to hurt you but you have hurt me. He held my face between his hands, kissed me gently, then pressured me with his mouth as if he wanted to pry me open. "I like you so much," he said. "I wish I could crawl inside you and stay there for a very long time."

I now understand why it is that I have not been kissed until my eighteenth year. I am convinced that had I been kissed earlier I never would have studied for my SAT's. I also know that now that I *have* been kissed it is anybody's guess whether I graduate from high school. And my leukemia seems nothing more than God's way of keeping men out of my life.

For the record, there was absolutely no lip fuzz involved.

I am a tough customer, despite my lack of experience. And the only thing I noted, which might qualify as a complaint, and which I later discussed with Lenore at great length —without compromising my source—is that I could feel things go out of control south of Jonathan's belt. I did nothing to warrant this, and it made me feel unneeded—as if Jonathan's body could not distinguish between a young woman and an oak tree he might find himself rubbing against.

As a general rule I like a man with more restraint, though Lenore says young men cannot help themselves. "When that little soldier stands up," she says, "there is nothing they can do."

Which explains why so many men my age wear raincoats on sunny days.

9.

Mortal Sins

Since last night, mouths have become an obsession: Grace's —tough and wrinkled as beef jerky; Lenore's—thin and colorless as a rubber band; Leo's—pale and predictable as a greeting card; Mr. Welsh's—moist as an earthworm; Maria's—smooth as porcelain; mine—perfection; Custer's—generous enough to invite kissing; Jonathan's—very good indeed, but UGH!

Does kissing Jonathan make me a slut?

All of a sudden I do not want *anyone* to know. I do not even want Jonathan to remember the incident, but how do you make someone forget something that has already become a cherished memory, a memory they would bronze like a baby shoe if they could?

Custer is back from his canoe trip. His arms are very sore because Carmencita did not paddle once—not even once. As they pulled into our driveway, I could read Custer's bad mood through the windshield; his eyes and mouth were fixed on a horizontal, immovable as the equator, and Carmencita, who was talking and gesturing madly, did not seem to be able to interest Custer in her conversation.

I was sitting on the porch finishing my story for this week's *Chronicle*, which will come out late because, as most of our subscribers know, the Editor in Chief is screwing the Sales Manager of the paper.

"How was it?"

"How was what?"

"The trip?"

Custer glanced over his shoulder to make sure Carmencita could not hear what he was about to say. "Let's just say . . ." He noticed Grace crossing the living room. She had put on her best sandals to greet him. "Let's just say that sometimes you gotta take the good with the bad." He kissed Grace on both cheeks and looked back toward his Thunderbird. "I shouldn't keep Carmencita waiting. Do you guys have stories ready?"

Grace said she had a column on flea collars for pets.

Dog-killer! I felt like yelling.

"I'm finishing an article on your mother's new dance studio. She's decided she wants to teach."

"Yeah. I know—*plié*, *relevé*, and all that crap," he said, benignly mocking his mother's deep Southern accent. He pirouetted his way back to the car, spinning dizzily until he crashed against his own fender and landed hip first on our blacktop. After picking himself up, he smiled, tucked his T-shirt into his jeans, and shouted, "I'll come by and get your stuff this afternoon."

Carmencita waved good-bye, not in the Miss America way this time—more like the Queen of England when she raises her arm and twists her cupped hand like a sleepy periscope.

Custer will get my story when I am good and ready.

Maria—who has still not given up on me—needs me to tape a second show for Mr. Welsh this afternoon.

Mr. Welsh called the minute we had returned from the studio this morning. He told Maria we needed a backup program because he would be traveling next week, and might not make it back in time for the live show next Sunday.

This is a bald-faced lie because Mr. Welsh always makes his way home on weekends. Custer even told me that before his parents got married certain things were negotiated; and one of them required Mr. Welsh to reserve weekends for his family. In fact, Custer says his stepfather is excessively proud of the fact that, however crazy his week has been and wherever he may find himself on Fridays—in Europe or as far away as Alaska—he has never spent a weekend away from home.

We are taping an extra show this afternoon because Mr. Welsh concocts fourteen hundred reasons to see or talk to Maria, hoping that one of them, like this one, will pan out. In a different but almost similar way, I take fifteen hundred books out of the Mainsfield library, hoping that one of them will be worthwhile. They have put me on the "Chronic Abusers List" because we have a local librarian who discourages reading. Kitty Hart sits in her office, jabbering on the phone; and while doing so, she scans her files, picks out the people who read too much, adds them to the Chronic Abusers List, and prepares OVERDUE notices for her next mailing.

Mr. Welsh is becoming a chronic abuser of a different sort.

Yesterday's interview with Mrs. Welsh gave me my first glimpse of life inside the Welsh castle. I had never really spent any time with Mrs. Welsh and her black poodle, Rufus-Coco, because Custer always preferred to come over to our house.

Rufus-Coco is a sex maniac. He does not discriminate between animals and people. One day he is after Lafayette and the next he is after me. Walking into the Welsh castle, I was greeted by Mrs. Welsh in a pink leotard and toe shoes, as well as by Rufus-Coco, who immediately clamped his jaw on the shoelace of my sneaker and pulled me down a dark hallway.

"He's very playful," Mrs. Welsh said apologetically. Then she stood on toe as her enormous poodle forced himself behind me, sidestepping and scooping me down the hall toward the master bedroom. "Just follow him around a bit, and he'll leave you alone," she said.

I ended up in Custer's temporary bedroom, a simple room painted blue, with Bruce Springsteen, a Red Sox pennant, and a tourist map of Grenada on the walls. A set of *World Book* encyclopedias from Custer's father dominated the walnut bookcase. Above them was the *Spanish in a Nutshell* Custer had often consulted in the early days of his courtship with Carmencita; and beneath the encyclopedias, an entire shelf was devoted to Grenada: *Delta Forces in Grenada, The 82nd Airborne, St. George's Medical School.*

I peeked inside the last book, a government document called *After-Action Report.* Most of the pages had been blacked out. And just as I was trying to read what Custer had scribbled in the margins, I noticed a small black book—an artist's sketchbook—on his bedside table. I put down the *After-Action Report,* knowing I was about to do something very wrong. I opened the little black book—and right on the inside cover were the letters R.M.P. Underneath Custer had written: Respect My Privacy.

My face instantly burned with shame. I felt Custer in the room. But calm down, he *isn't*, I reassured myself. I flipped to the first page and looked at the date. The first entry had been made one year ago, when he and Carmencita had started to date.

I am not a masochist. I did not want to read anything gooey about Carmencita. I wanted to know, but then again I did not want to know, what Custer thought about *me*. I heard Rufus-Coco approaching, and with even greater speed I rifled through the pages of Custer's journal. Finally I came across my nickname. And, of course, at precisely that moment Rufus-Coco saw fit to attack my shoelaces. His jaw, a canine shredding machine, was busily turning my laces into wet linguini. I shook him off brutally, but the dog was so persistent, I barely had time to make out the following:

> Don't know what to think about Red.
> Carmencita still in the picture, but
> Red confuses me lately and is
> growing up to be a great beauty.

Rufus-Coco snatched the book out of my hands—shoelaces no longer holding any fascination for him—and I found myself pleading with the great black poodle. No teeth, *please!* I dug into my pocket and handed him the Kit-Kat Maria had bought me earlier in the day. I ripped off the wrapper, waved the Kit-Kat around, and pretended I was about to swallow the chocolate wafer whole. Rufus-Coco dropped the book, sprang up on his hind legs, and displayed a singularity of purpose I had seen only once before in my life—from his owner, Mark Welsh. I secured Custer's book with my foot, and dropped the Kit-Kat directly into Rufus-Coco's mouth.

Fortunately, the book had neither been damaged nor slobbered upon. I was tempted to read on, but before I knew it, Rufus-Coco had maneuvered me down another corridor into the master bedroom.

When the furry beast had successfully forced me into the (knowing-what-I-think-I-know) loveless chamber, he jumped up big as a bear and pinned me against the bed with all fours. He licked my face, slobbered all over my person, and grew more and more excited in ways that altogether compromised my visit.

"Rufus-Coco—*stop that!*" Mrs. Welsh shouted, emerging from the hall on toe. "He must be starving," she said—again, apologetically—as she came down from the relevé.

"Rufus-Coco—*tenderloin!*"

The stupid glutton withdrew his affection as brusquely as he had offered it. Then he jumped off the bed, scrambled toward the kitchen, and claimed his meat from Mrs. Welsh, who—characteristically, I was beginning to learn—met this and all of life's more dramatic moments on toe.

Louisa Welsh might not be as bad as I thought. For one thing, she is Custer's mother. And the revelation that Custer is not indifferent to me made me thaw in the presence of anyone associated with him.

By way of background, I learned that Louisa Fourchette was born to a local judge in Mississippi. While visiting her Aunt Louella in Fayetteville, North Carolina, seventeen-year-old Louisa met George V. Daniels—who had grown up in the town of Aiken, Mississippi.

George and Louisa raised Custer in Fayetteville, where

George had started boot camp. "George said I was the only woman in Fayetteville who did not have a tattoo of a Harley-Davidson on my breast and chew tobacco," Louisa recalled. In 1972, one year after Custer was born, George narrowly escaped being sent to Quang Tri along with hundreds of Rangers who had never seen combat.

Louisa comes from a small town near Jackson. "So small," she says, "the town hall is a trailer." Aiken, whose population boasts ten people more than its neighbor, shares the town hall with Pine Grove.

When Louisa went back for her father's funeral in May 1982, the Fourchette family papers could not be found. Boo-Ray Clarkson, the town's seventy-six-year-old clerk, had authorized four generations of Pine Grove records to be stored in the basement of the local Baptist church while a new trailer was being equipped with air-conditioning. One day before the funeral, while Boo-Ray's wife Tulah was guarding the records and ironing her funeral dress at the same time, she accidentally set fire to the basement of the church. Since Tulah was the only black woman in the county married to a white man, the town marshal spread rumors about a black conspiracy to destroy white history. Louisa's theory is that the town marshal is a rat. She claims her father's body was not even cold when Marshal Marshall came to the door with daffodils for her mother.

"*Un vieux gigolo,*" I said.

"Pardon?"

"That's what Mrs. Pederson calls Mr. Sneff."

"The grocer?"

"Yeah—a fortune hunter. He's after Grace."

We chatted a while, then I asked, "How did Mr. Daniels

die?" It sounded a little sudden, but in the context of her father's death, it did not seem indecent.

"Well, I'd rather not go into it, Meredith. It's all speculation anyway."

I was sorry I had asked, but she continued answering the question.

"We'd lived apart since Custer was ten, and the only times I saw George Daniels were on the occasions he picked Custer up to take him fishing. His mom told me he died in combat. The other day she sent me a letter I haven't even opened. She put Custer's name on the envelope, so I passed it on to him."

"Custer's been trying to sort it all out."

"I can't blame him."

"Don't you want to know?"

"Honey, that man gave me so much grief while he was alive! I can't honestly say I was sorry to see him go. But he loved me. That much I'll give him. He loved me to distraction. And since he loved Custer, I did my best not to interfere with that love."

Had I come from Louisa Fourchette's part of the world, I might very well have put on toe shoes and danced my way to Atlanta, then to New York. Along the way she had stopped in Memphis for a date with Elvis. Louisa showed me the eight-by-ten photograph of them together (the only bit of Elvis memorabilia Mr. Welsh had *not* appropriated for Maria). As winner of the Mississippi Sweet Sixteen Dance Contest, she had flown in Elvis's private plane and eaten dinner with him.

Mrs. Welsh stretches her vowels lengthwise. Her voice muscles are as carefully trained as her leg muscles, which, despite her forty years, are still as shapely as those of a thirty-year-old ballerina. Mrs. Pederson gets a kick out of the way Mrs. Welsh pronounces her ballet terms. ***Plié, relevé,*** and ***pas de bourré*** should not end in as many A's—"plea-aaaye, rella-vaaaye, podda-boo-raaaye."

Northerners sometimes assume accented individuals are stupid, which is a mistake. I confess that until I interviewed Louisa I thought she was dumb, but not because of her accent; I had just assumed that Mr. Welsh would marry a stupid woman, and I was wrong.

Mrs. Welsh demonstrated her positions at the barre. She showed me around her new dance studio—which looked so convincing with barres and mirrors I almost forgot that it had been Custer's bedroom.

"I will conduct two sets of classes," Mrs. Welsh said, suddenly talking in a crisp businesswoman's Southern. "One for serious dancers, which I will call the Master Class; the other for dancers with little or no experience. 'The Welsh Technique' will combine the masterful example of my great teacher Balanchine with the personal experience I have gained in a career devoted to dance."

Only when she talked like a press release did I find Mrs. Welsh vain and pretentious. I am sympathetic to the fact that Mrs. Welsh is bored, and that because her husband travels a great deal she is trying to make something of herself. But I liked her better after we had wrapped up the dance demonstration. She briefly started talking about Custer. "He's my hope and prayer, that boy." She popped down off her toes. "And don't think I don't notice what a good friend you are to him, Meredith."

I also noticed how much Custer resembles his mother. Their coloring is different (she has dyed her hair blonde), but their features are similar—somehow delicate and generous at the same time. By that I mean there are no excess lines; yet at no point do you leave the face feeling deprived.

Custer has arrived to pick up our stories. He is looking at me differently. Everybody seems to be looking at me with a strange expression except Grace who is re-reading Mr. Sneff's love letter, with a smile creeping upon her face.

"Whatchya got there, Gracie?" Custer asked.

"Oh, a letter from an admirer," she said coyly.

"Gonna marry you?"

"I expect so. Needs a lesson in handling money, though . . ."

"The good Lord put you on this earth to teach us all, Gracie."

She smiled.

"Meredith!"

Maria was calling me.

"Custer," I said, "Here's the story. I think Maria's ready to leave—your dad wants to do a second show today."

"Phone! For you—it's Jonathan!"

I broke into a cold sweat, and poked my head through the doorway which separates the porch from the living room. "Tell him I'm not here!" I mouthed the words so that Jonathan could not possibly hear me.

Only when I heard the words "I'm sorry Jonathan, Meredith isn't here at the moment" did I relax.

Custer was smiling because he had heard everything. He saw how uncomfortable I was and now he thinks he's got stuff on me.

"Has Jonathan been serenading you while I've been away?"

"You dog!" I said.

"Was he any good?"

"Was *she* any good?"

Custer was offended by my counterattack. But I cannot help it. When my moon is in Scorpio, that is what happens.

I stared at Custer long enough for him to read the words SHUT UP! on my pupils. Custer knows I am less experienced than he. And he knows that I am extremely sensitive about it. When I lost a year at school it was not because someone like Custer was poking me in the back seat of a Thunderbird!

"Are you my friend?" I asked Custer.

"Yes," he said.

"Are you my best friend?" I asked. My face was on fire.

"Yes," he repeated.

"Then shut up," I said.

Custer looked very hurt.

Tough! I was too.

There is an arrogance in the way he and Carmencita make you feel that you are not an adult, or that you are missing something essential in life *just* because you have not rubbed up against a naked individual while you yourself are naked.

I did not want to cry in front of Custer, so I ran through the house, out the back door, and sat on the grass next to the spot in the pond which had swallowed Mr. Welsh's letter. I watched dragonflies shiver the surface of the water and heard frogs plop in from unseen mud caves. Lafayette romped over from her lawn, leaping over patches of black-eyed Susans. She started licking the hot salty wash that was brimming from my eyes. I pushed her away.

I cannot not understand why things have changed since Carmencita and Jonathan have come into the picture. I do not want anything to change, but when I look at things squarely I see that they have. A whole new set of considerations, less neat and less honest, have come into play since Custer and I have widened our social circle beyond each other.

Part Two

Geography of a Soul

Nor would a snapshot reveal a halo

—W. H. Auden, "Insignificant Elephants"

10.

Boxer Shorts and Beach Vacations

Jonathan has offered to get me out of here. So has Mr. Welsh. Not directly, but through Maria. He has rented a house on Cape Cod for a week in order to celebrate the success of the business show. The whole thing hinges on Maria. If she declines, I will not see the ocean this summer.

I hope Maria decides to go. Leo disappointed her again, promising he would visit, then calling at the last minute to say that he might not be able to take the last week in August off. An emergency came up: his consulting firm assigned him to a food company which is having trouble with its whipping cream division. In midair, somewhere over Wichita, he said, all the plastic containers of Tasti-Whip had exploded under pressure. New packaging for air shipping is being developed.

I hope Leo's hometown smothers under the goop that fell from the sky. And I am sorry I ever asked for his telephone number. Leo's penny loafers, his navy blue sports jacket, the way he opens doors for Maria and all that Ivy League crap is beginning to wear thin. Besides, I am told he wears boxer shorts. (Custer says the world is divided into two types of men —those who wear boxer shorts and those who wear briefs.)

Leo does not even bother to defend himself. "In Wichita,"

he says, "hard work makes an honorable man." Maria says Leo smiles when he pronounces these platitudes. But I think he holds fast to his Midwest frame of reference, taking Wichita with him wherever he goes.

Not even Maria has succeeded in rattling a self-possession which, however foolish to the rest of us, seems to give order to Leo's life. Today, on the anniversary of their meeting last August, Maria conceded that Leo is in a different orbit, not subject to any electrical charges or gravitational pulls—be they emotional or circumstantial. He has a built-in circuit breaker; and when the current from people—particularly from passionate women like Maria—gets too strong, the boy from Kansas shuts down.

The citizens who leave Kansas seem very ambitious and, when they get to New York, Maria says they are even more aggressive than the natives. Maria is convinced Leo was hired for his brains, but also because he is a can-do person who works on Thanksgiving and New Year's to show his allegiance to the firm.

Lenore, who always offers an opinion on any crisis to strike at the bosom of our family, thinks Leo is in his "I'm a genius" phase. She reminded us of his behavior on New Year's Eve. Rather than drink champagne with Maria, Leo accepted another "emergency" assignment. So when Maria called in tears last New Year's Eve because Leo had just telephoned to say that he had to work until the ball dropped in Times Square, Lenore, thinking she was consoling Maria, told her to forget "that prep school ass-kisser." Even Custer had gotten on the phone; he tried to make Maria laugh by telling her that men who wore boxer shorts were wimps.

In a way, I hope Maria accepts Mr. Welsh's vacation offer, even if he is married. At least he loves her. I have no idea what Mr. Welsh has said to Mrs. Welsh on the subject of Cape Cod. All I know is that Grace has started packing. Mr. Welsh invited Grace, thinking it would make Maria happy.

Mark Welsh became more aggressive about the trip after he found out Maria had "a houseguest" coming the last week in August. Last Sunday he confronted my sister.

"Houseguest? How can you have a houseguest if you don't own a goddamn house!" Mr. Welsh got so worked up his microphone popped out from behind his tie. "Where's he going to sleep?"

"I'm not answering these questions."

"I'm insanely jealous!"

"You have no right to be."

"Who is this guy?" I could hear it all through my headphones.

"I didn't say it was a guy."

"Who is he?"

"FIVE MINUTES TO AIR—STAND BY!" Danny Dorino shouted over the paging system.

"It doesn't concern you."

"What's his name?"

"None of your business."

"Saunders—If you don't tell me I'll ask you in front of thirty million viewers!"

Mr. Welsh rarely called Maria by her last name. When he did, it was his humorous way of being serious. And it usually worked.

"Leo."

"Leo who?"

"Leo. What does it matter what his name is?"

"I only know one goddamn Leo and I want to make sure he's not the one."

"You know this is really none of your business." She pointed to Mr. Welsh's wedding ring.

"I love you, dammit! It *is* my business. This Leo doesn't work in consulting, does he?"

"No."

"TWO MINUTES TO AIR—STAND BY!"

"He's not from Kansas, is he?"

"No."

"LIVE FROM WFUW—THE MARK WELSH BUSINESS HOUR!"

Maria left the floor. When she walked into the control room, our eyes locked.

"Jesus," I said.

Maria ignored me and pointed to the monitor. As we watched Mr. Welsh open the show with his Business Summary, Maria said, "He doesn't look worried."

"Why should he be? You lied to him."

"Oh come on! How many Leos from Kansas work in New York consulting firms?"

"Not too many. Why didn't you tell him the truth?"

"Shock, I guess. Besides, it's none of his business."

"Jesus," I said. Then I paused to give full weight to the horror of the situation.

The only thing holding me back from Mr. Welsh's trip is my commitment to *The Highland Chronicle*, a commitment Grace does not seem to share. When I finally discussed the trip with

Custer, who has been trying to get a hold of me since he hurt my feelings, he said not to worry about *The Chronicle*. "If anyone gave me a choice between *The Chronicle* and a week on the dunes in Provincetown, I know what I'd choose," he said. And in fact, he had chosen. Custer was going too. He apologized for ribbing me last week. "You wanna talk about it?" I said no.

I will talk with Custer when events turn so as to give me a strategic advantage. I do not want sympathy. I want leverage. Until then I have decided to let things slide. Even Custer's college entrance exams are less a concern of mine. We took the SAT's last week, and while I think I did reasonably well, Custer is convinced he did not break 1200.

As for Carmencita, I have no desire to slug it out with her. But I have realized that the less I worry about Custer, the more I see him as a young man worth pursuing. When I am sufficiently repelled by the ever-constant Jonathan, I remind myself that Custer asked me to be his girlfriend first.

The heat is unbearable today. I am spending the morning in our backyard, where even the tiger lilies have fainted. Only the skunk cabbage looks alert.

Grace remains on the porch. That's the plan. She has stopped using Kleenex to dab her armpits, preferring Bounty paper towels for the real scorchers. The television commercial showed a cross-section of the paper they use, magnified a thousand times. Grace watched it, and immediately called her personal grocer. Within the hour, Mr. Sneff delivered a box of Bounty, along with a case of Grace's favorite mineral water.

This morning the ants are on parade, carrying bits of bark,

leaf cuttings, and marching to God knows where. As I leaned over to inspect, another set of tiny creatures fizzed up my nose like seltzer live from a glass. Dancing gnats. I hate them. Lafayette is chasing butterflies, crouching in a ready position, and leaping over clusters of black-eyed Susans whenever she sees a Monarch. She loves our pond, and will jump in to fetch sticks, tennis balls, or lesser prizes. Afterwards, she comes over to me, dripping with water and sediment, and shakes herself more forcefully than our dryer on Final Spin.

Just as I had recovered from one such assault, I heard a voice above me call, "Meredith. Honey, wake up! Make room for your grandmother." When I opened my eyes, I saw two large white crescents, which came into focus as the rubber toes of Grace's tennis shoes. "Get up!" she said. "There's plenty of room on that blanket for me. Better yet, get your grandmother a chair."

I am docile when I first wake. So it took me a while before I said, "It's too hot for you out here, Grace."

"Nonsense," she said.

"It's very buggy," I insisted.

"I brought my gauze," she said.

I swam out of my slothfulness and looked up to see Grace's upside-down face, blocking the sun. Her safari hat and veil and the sharp black form poking out from her waist made an ominous silhouette. "I bought this for my trip to the Amazon," she said, referring to her headgear. "Never used it. Irving chickened out."

"What's that other thing?"

"*The Purple Land.*"

"Who wrote it?"

"Same one who wrote that book on Patagonia I gave you. W. H. Hudson."

Suddenly Grace asked, "Where's Custer?"

"Don't know."

"Why not? You always know each other's whereabouts."

"Not anymore."

"Is he still dating that little beauty from Nicaragua?"

"She's a big beauty, and her name is Carmencita. She's only half Nicaraguan. The other side is Cuban."

"Well, then he's got his hands full. What about that lovely stepfather of his? What's he up to?"

"Planning for Cape Cod."

"I'm ready. I was invited, you know. He called right after your father rang from the south of France last week."

"What was the name of that cathedral with the gargoyles they loved?"

"Dijon."

"That's right."

"We'll have Mr. Welsh to thank if he gets us out of this tar pit. Your father never warned me how hot it gets."

I got Grace a chair from the basement, the hardest one I could find. I carried up a beach umbrella as well. That way no one will blame me if Grace drops dead from a sunstroke.

Grace put on her glasses and opened her book. She told me that she had read it four times and would never tire of it. Five minutes into reading, I heard the sound of monotone grunting at regular intervals. I looked up, half-expecting to see Mrs. Pederson leading a baby pig around our lawn in search of truffles. But it was Grace, page-deep in low-grade laughter.

"Meredith, honey—listen to this."

I stared at the ant trail, a caravan of insects one hundred strong, and listened to Grace read her favorite passage.

> What the deuce was that? My sleepy soliloquy was suddenly brought to a most lame and impotent conclusion for I had heard a sound of terror—the unmistakable zz-zzing of an insect's wings. It was the hateful vinchuca.

"Ouch!" I shouted.

"What's the matter?"

"Thought I'd been bitten, that's all."

"This vinchuca's in Argentina. He can't bother you."

> It can fly, and in a dark room know where to find you. Having selected a nice tender part, it pierces the skin with its proboscis or rostrum, and sucks vigorously for two or three minutes . . .

"Yikes!" This time I screamed. Surely I had been bitten.

"What is it now?"

"Horsefly, or maybe worse." I was fidgety. My blood seemed just beneath my pores, vulnerable to attack by any creature, the smaller, the more loathsome.

> Strange to say, you do not feel the operation, even when lying wide awake. By that time the creature, so attenuated before, has assumed the figure, size, and general appearance of a ripe gooseberry, so much blood has it drawn from your veins . . .

"AAAAUGH! A wasp! A yellow jacket!"

"Did it sting you?"

"Not yet!" I jumped up, grabbed *The Purple Land*, and tried to slam the book shut every time the wobbly yellow craft came within range. Grace objected to her book being used that way. "W. H. Hudson would have wanted it!" I exclaimed. Finally I sat still with the book splayed open on the vinchuca page. I finished the passage for Grace, interrupting myself once when, out of the corner of my eye, I saw the winged killer flying precariously close to Lafayette's pink and slumbering belly.

> That the pain should come after and not during the operation is an arrangement very advantageous to the vinchuca.

Just then, the yellow jacket was hovering approximately four inches above Lafayette's nipple. *THWUMP!*

I had done it. Lafayette was barking her throat off.

"I saved your life, you ungrateful mutt!" I screamed at Lafayette. I was just as unnerved as she.

"Let me see!" Grace shouted with excitement. I handed Grace the book. I did not want to look. "I'm sorry," I said. "I'll buy you another copy." Grace opened the book, crinkling her nose at first, then smiled as if she had committed the murder and were privately delighting in it.

The chrome bridge chair was a mistake. Grace could not sleep. It forced her to sit up straight and talk. When Lafayette had stopped barking, Grace returned to the subject of my friend, ex-best friend—I don't know what to call Custer.

"Let me tell you something about men, Meredith, honey. They'll get it where they can get it. Even nice boys like Custer. Why buy the cow if the milk is free?"

"He asked me first."

"What?"

"To be his girlfriend."

"Oh. But he doesn't want you that way—"

"Let's talk about something else." I did not want to be insulted.

"No. Let's finish up—"

"Let's not." I stood up. "Lenore's calling me."

"Sit down and let me finish!" Grace ordered. I had never heard her so focused. "I'm not deaf yet, and Lenore didn't call you."

"I truly believe that Harold was in love with me until the day he died."

I did not comment, except to ask with strained politeness who Harold was.

"You know, the one I used to take care of at the hospital."

"The one with everything sticking out?"

"That's right."

"The one who gave you your first kiss?"

"Exactly." She was quiet for a moment, and I sat down, reluctantly. "Now the reason I never fell in love with Harold is that he was always sick. Even as a boy. Poor fellow always had a massive cold when everyone else just had the sniffles."

"What does this have to do with—"

"What I'm saying is that Harold was always sick. I knew I was the kind of woman who could not love a man who caught every bug that came along. I loved him, I pitied him, and in the end I was the only one left to take care of him."

I stood up again. I had a queasy feeling that things could only get worse.

"Young lady, sit down and hear me out."

Grace grabbed me with her arm, sharp as a chicken wing.

"Custer's seen you sick, very sick. He lost his father when

he was twelve and he doesn't want to lose you."

"*I'm not sick!*" I yelled so hard Lafayette gave me a you've-really-lost-it-now look and jumped into the pond.

"Calm down! For God's sake, Meredith, calm down! I know you're not sick—"

"WELL THEN SHUT UP!"

I could not endure another word.

11.

The Zipper and Surprise Visits

Maria said yes to Mr. Welsh and ever since the Alphabet Streets exist only to suggest the better place we are going to. A storm last night rinsed off our world, but somehow I am seeing another landscape. Instead of corn, I see dune grass opposite our porch. Instead of terrarium air, I am whiffing a brisker, saltier molecule. No tar bubbles under my feet. Only grains of sand.

I went to the mall with Lenore, who is not coming with us, and shopped for a new bathing suit.

"Try something bold for a change. The white one with the cheetah dots on it."

"Too vulgar." I pointed to the large white zipper on the side of the bathing suit. "And too high cut in the legs."

"Try it on. You can get away with it. And Custer would approve." She laughed and brought over two bikinis the size of postage stamps. "Forget those," I said. "Give me the cheetah."

When Lenore heard the metallic ripping sound of curtain rings, she turned and watched me emerge from the fitting room.

"I like it on you!"

"I don't."

"Why?"

"It clashes with my hair."

"Stop that. It suits you."

The saleslady came by. I was thinking that she had better not give me some crap about how cute the bathing suit looks.

"That looks *cute* on you!" she said.

I pretended I was not listening. "How do you work the zipper?"

"Like this." The saleswoman pulled the white plastic ring down my left side, stopping at my hip. "If I go any further, the whole thing'll come off."

Lenore smiled. "It's very classy. Even with the zipper."

"Definitely," the saleswoman added. "Clean lines. Nice scoop in the back." She turned me around so that I could look at myself in the three-way mirror. "Just make sure the boys keep their hands off the zipper."

Ha ha ha. I hate the way salespeople assume that air of instant intimacy when they are confident they have made a sale.

I bought the suit. All day long I secretly tried it on in my room, modeling it in front of the mirror, zipping it up and down to Bruce Springsteen singing "Tougher than the Rest." I even imagined someone ripping it off me—"*All you gotta do is say yes!*"

While I was putting on my shorts, I saw Mr. Welsh crossing the Pedersons' lawn. He was on his way to our house and I was nervous. Mr. Welsh never comes over. Maria was home, but she was on the phone with Leo. Her door was closed in an unfriendly way, as if Shoot to Kill were written on one of those hotel cards you hang on the doorknob.

Mr. Welsh was holding a letter and something I could not identify.

"Anybody home?"

I tucked in my shirt and went downstairs.

"Lenore, are you home?"

It made perfect sense to ask for the person who *least* wanted to see you. If Lenore were a horse, Mr. Welsh would have offered her sugar.

"She's not here."

"Hi, Ace!" Mr. Welsh smiled and looked relieved. "Is our boss-woman here?"

"She's on the phone with a friend from New York."

"Oh."

I could have said something about Leo. "She doesn't love him" is what he wanted to hear. But I let him sweat it out. The result was that Mr. Welsh looked demoralized, though, I must say, very trim and handsome.

"Would you mind giving this stuff to Maria?"

He handed me a letter and a baseball. A real one. Made in Haiti. At the same time, I saw Carmencita coming toward our porch. She waved at me and, just as Mr. Welsh caught sight of her, he raised his voice, "So be sure to tell Maria that I'll need two half-inch copies of last week's show. My wife wants to send them to her relatives in Mississippi."

Carmencita beamed at me and Mr. Welsh. She kissed me on both cheeks and had so much love and goodwill left over I thought she would burst out of her floral sundress.

Mr. Welsh gave a polite hello to Carmencita and she immediately gushed with thanks for Mr. Welsh's invitation to Cape Cod. Mr. Welsh shuffled around like a big altar boy in tennis whites (when he is not performing, Mr. Welsh's social skills are mostly inept) and then he returned to his castle.

Carmencita came out back with me. She braided black-eyed Susans and chattered with excitement. "Custer says there's a house on the dunes owned by the national parks and it's so isolated people ride on horseback at sunset!" Carmencita finished the garland and exclaimed. "I can't *wait!*"

I had not expected Carmencita's visit and was at a loss for small talk.

"I bought a bathing suit," I said. I did not describe it. I would not tell her where I had bought it. Carmencita did not want to talk about bathing suits. "I'm too fat," she said. Then she asked me what I was reading.

"A book about Argentina Grace gave me," I showed her the jacket. Grace had recently covered *The Purple Land* with clear Contac paper. That same day she had cleaned up the vinchuca page with a Handi-Wipe.

"In Spanish?"

"English. It was written by an Englishman who lived there."

"Oh. But what does an Englishman know about South America?"

"Don't know. Haven't read it yet. I think he knows a lot about the natural life there."

"Like what?"

"Bugs and stuff. Grace read me a passage about a bug called the vinchuca. It was funny."

"The kind of bug that bites you and you fall in love?"

Suddenly I was envious. Carmencita and I had been having a pleasant conversation. There was no need for her to remind me that she was in love.

"Is that what happened to you?"

"What?"

"A bug bit you and you fell in love?"

"I'm not in love."

"What do you mean you're not in love?"

"Just what I said. I'm not in love."

"What about—" I checked myself. "You know what?—it's really none of my business." I closed my eyes and pretended I was trying to sleep.

"Sure it is."

"No. It's not."

"It *is* your business because you're in love. You're in love with Custer."

My eyes popped open to read Carmencita's face. Her tone had been very matter of fact, without the slightest hint of provocation. Her face held no malice.

"You can have him," she said. "He's yours!" Then Carmencita started that hand-waving business, as she always does when she wants to make a point. *"Demasiado serio para mi!"*

"What's that supposed to mean?"

"It means he's too serious for me."

Carmencita rolled on her side to look at me. We were lying on the grass which was hot with sun and spongy underneath from last night's rainfall. She propped herself up on her elbow, which sank into the ground a little. Carmencita stifled a scream.

My entire body jumped at the sound of Carmencita's cry. "What's the matter?"

"I hate it when the ground sinks suddenly! Like in graveyards. Ever notice how the ground is always moist and sqwooshy in graveyards?"

"Shut up!" I shuddered. "You're giving me goose bumps."

"Can't help it," Carmencita smiled. "Custer's always trying to figure out how his father died." She looked like a young Elizabeth Taylor when she smiled.

"You love Custer, don't you?" she asked.

"He's my best friend. Or he was until recently."

"That's not what I mean. You *love* him, don't you?"

"What do you mean?"

"You think about him with his clothes off."

"Never."

"Yes you do!"

"Nope."

"You think about him with his shirt off—"

"Never."

"You think about him with his jeans off—"

"No!"

"You wonder what it would be like to have his mouth gently sucking at your breast—"

"No—never!"

Carmencita nudged my shoulder. "Come on Meredith—admit it! You're lying to me and you *know* it!"

"I'm *not* lying." I could not suppress my smile. That witch noticed immediately.

"You see! You *are* lying—I knew it!"

"I'm *not* lying." I folded my smile and put it away. She really was amazing. Carmencita could bore a hole down to the place a person's innermost thoughts were stored.

"Well then, if you're not lying, you don't know what you want. And you *should* know. If you *do* want him, then you should *fight* for what you want! Not up here—" She pointed to my head. "Down here!" She smacked her chest over what she thought was her heart.

I smiled and moved her hand to the left side of her chest.

Carmencita laughed and started hitting the other side of her chest. *"Tu tienes que saber lo que tu quieres."*

"Talk English! You're in America. And don't hit yourself so hard. You'll break something."

"All I said was, 'You must know what you want.'"

"Oh yeah? And what do you want?"

"What do you mean?"

"Que quieres?" I said, testing the one phrase I had picked up from Custer's *Spanish in a Nutshell.*

"Muy bien!" She popped up off her elbow and applauded my effort. Her hands were wild as leaves being stirred in a street wind. All in all, Carmencita was being rather sweet and disarming.

"I can give you Jonathan," I said, doing my best to stay serious. When I saw Carmencita's face breaking at the seams, I myself erupted into Maria-type laughter.

Carmencita screamed with pleasure. "HA! HA! You know, HA! He's really not so bad! HA-HA-HA!"

Her mascara was running all over the place. She sighed, relaxed her laughter, and wiped her cheeks in order to inspect exactly how much Maybelline had ended up on her face. When she turned her black palms toward me, I looked at her face, which was still a grey smear. "You look like Ash Wednesday!" I said. Another burst of laughter from Carmencita. But shortly thereafter she got serious. "Let's not talk about the church," she said. Right away I knew that Carmencita's laughter had been less a reflection of my wit than of her audacious relationship with an institution I knew governed her family's life.

Lafayette pawed and sniffed her way over to us. She was fresh from the pond and her coat had settled on her underbelly like a long wet eyelash.

"So what *do* you want?"

"Me?"

"No—Lafayette." I stopped to pat Lafayette, who mistook my affection for a signal to shake her considerable portion of pond water all over us. "Yes, *you!*" I said, removing a clump of leaf mulch from the corner of my mouth.

"I want to give you Custer—"

"I don't believe this! And what makes you think I want him?"

"I just do. I think you're well matched. Besides, that's what they do in Ethiopia."

"What?"

"If a relationship is not working out, it's the obligation of the person leaving the relationship to introduce the person being left to another friend. Someone you trust. And I trust you, Meredith. You're my friend."

I wondered what I had done to deserve Carmencita's friendship. "Jesus Christ, Carmencita! You're really bizarre."

"Why?"

"Because you're so detached!"

"No I'm not!" She sat up and made me look at her. "Don't ever say that—I'm not at all detached!"

"Well, what am I supposed to think?

"I'm *not* detached. It's just that I'm not in love with Custer. And because you're my friend and I think you like him I want you to have him."

"I don't want him."

"He's a great lover—"

I really did not want to hear this. "Carmencita, I really don't want to hear—"

"—but I'm in love with someone else."

At this point, Custer seemed about as desirable as the dog food in the collection box at Mr. Sneff's supermarket.

"You know, Carmencita. I don't think I should be hearing all this. If I had wanted Custer I would have taken him when he asked me to be his girlfriend."

"When was that?"

"*Long* before he asked you." I sat on the word *long* for the better part of a generation.

Carmencita looked as if her head had been bitten off.

"I said he was a great—"

"I know what you said. Let me finish!" I had learned this command from Grace. And I could match Carmencita's earnestness any day. "The second thing is that I am still Custer's friend. So you tie me up in knots when you tell me you're in love with someone else. If I'm a good friend I should tell Custer!"

"A friend who wanted something other than friendship could use it to her advantage."

"That's sick."

"I'm just being honest with you."

"And you're assuming I want him."

I threw a rock into the pond and watched Lafayette jump after it. Her forceful wake upset the delicate rings my rock had brought to the surface.

"Custer's better for you, Meredith. I'm too shallow for him. He's always thinking about things. If I see one more book about the invasion of Grenada, I'm going to scream. That's where he is right now, you know."

"Grenada?"

"No. The library. He's filling out more requisition slips. Kitty Hart likes him."

"She *hates* me."

"Well, she likes Custer. She's already bought three books on Grenada just for him." Carmencita was quiet for a moment. "Meredith, I love Custer but he drags me down."

I secretly commended Carmencita for her extraordinary self-knowledge, then asked, "Who is this guy?"

"Which guy?"

"The one you're in love with."

Carmencita's face lit up. And even with watered-down mascara smeared all over her face, she looked very beautiful.

"Mark Welsh," she said.

12.

Carmencita Alfonso's Insanity

"ARE YOU CRAZY?" I shouted.

Carmencita jumped and the black-eyed Susans fell out of her hair.

"HAVE YOU LOST YOUR MIND!"

She was scared, initially, but my reaction was so unexpected Carmencita's fear quickly turned to laughter. She was doing her best to keep her cheeks from exploding.

"He's married! He's Custer's stepfather! And he's probably the fattest, most worthless mother's son that was ever born—"

"He's been losing weight!"

"Never mind that! He's still the most despicable stepfather ever to have walked the planet and possibly the universe. That no-good blubber-toad of a businessman-evangelist is not worth the tree bark Rufus-Coco pees on!"

"I think he's sexy."

"You're crazy."

"No I'm not. I watch the show and I think he's sexy."

"So's Custer."

"Yes," she said, catching my eye to let me know she was registering the remark as affirmation of our earlier conversation. "But his stepfather is sexy, smart, funny, and rich."

"And old."

"He's not that old."

"Jesus, Carmencita. He's forty-six!"

"So what?"

"So what? I'll tell you *so what.* Only whores and wives want forty-six year olds—that's what!"

"Well you asked me who my love was. And I told you. I think he's hot."

Carmencita started that dreamy talk. *Te amo, Marco, te amo con todo mi corazón!* I was thankful that, only a short time ago, she had restrained herself from a fuller expression of her love when she had joined Mr. Welsh and myself on the porch.

"Yeah, well you can forget about him."

Carmencita snapped out of her reverie. "Don't be so sure!" she said.

"I *know* you can forget about him."

"You think you know everything. *Pero tu no sabes nada!*"

I heard that.

What was I supposed to do? Divulge the numerous conversations I had heard on my headphones? Show Carmencita the teddy bears, the mugs, the sparkle pens, the books, the letters, the phone bills, and today's baseball? Our entire house has become a warehouse for Mark Welsh's affections.

What weird twist of head space constitutes Carmencita's brain! She arranges furniture up there in combinations no one would think up. And she lives up there, quite comfortably. When she takes the elevator and steps off at my floor, as she did today, Carmencita is exposed to different interiors, different ways of seeing. But it does not seem to rattle her.

I wonder what does rattle her.

13.

Grace Has Her Humanities and Custer's Search

Someone tore the stars out of the sky tonight. Clean rip. Forcing our attention down here on issues we least want to address. At least Maria is in a good mood. Leo said he was coming after all. "But I've made plans to go to Provincetown," Maria told him. Leo invited himself along.

Lenore thinks Maria gave in too easily. "That Leo thinks he can yell 'Timber!' and watch women fall," she said.

Maria is less and less interested in Lenore's opinions. "You've got to stop this, Lenore. You've got to stop assuming that all men are alike and that most men are like John."

"When I have evidence to the contrary, I will."

This is the closest Maria and Lenore get to fighting. Maria claimed Lenore does not give Leo a chance. She said Leo was under a lot of stress lately with his job. He has applied for a White House Fellowship because he wants to get out of consulting and is tired of all the Emergency assignments he is getting. When Maria said that Leo wanted more time to practice his piano, Lenore went berserk.

"His piano?" Lenore mocked with a quick laugh. "I love people like Leo. They discover that their job isn't all it's cracked up to be and decide they're too creative for what they're doing.

If they've saved enough money, then suddenly they're artists."

"He's not like that!" Maria protested.

"Oh yeah? John wasn't either."

"What's that supposed to mean?"

"After two years of business school and seven years as a trader, he suddenly announced that he had always wanted to write. The fact that he had never written a line in his life in no way discouraged him. Remember when he quit his job for a year?" Maria nodded. "During that period, he wrote some of the most aimless junk you've ever read. And the worst part of it was that I was the only one who would tell him the truth. All his friends told him his stuff was great. They were so frustrated with their own work, they pressured his efforts for their own sake—like stage mothers who had never made it! If you ask me, they were all cowards. John wasn't a coward. He just didn't have any talent. If Leo takes time off, he won't last more than two weeks with his piano."

"I'm not going to listen to this."

"Fine. Don't." Lenore shrugged her shoulders and walked into the kitchen.

"He's in love with you," Grace reassured Maria after Lenore was gone. "He wants to change his life because he's in love with you. That's what Mr. Welsh did when he met Louisa. He divorced his first wife for Louisa."

"His first wife?" Maria had a hard time concealing her shock.

"Mr. Welsh was married once before?" I asked. This was the first time I had spoken to Grace since our spat.

"No. You're right, Meredith. Must have been his second." Grace nodded toward me. "Louisa told me but I forgot."

I have to trust that two consultants will not slug it out over

Maria on the dunes in Provincetown. I want to believe that marriage will restrain Mr. Welsh as much as Leo's polite origins will have him resort to whatever they do in Wichita. I do not know what they do in Wichita. Probably challenge each other to a duel. Or maybe a genteel pheasant hunt followed by a homicide.

When relations between people get complicated and make me uneasy, people like Jonathan look significantly better. Just before nightfall, Jonathan arrived with *Camelot*, Grace's favorite album. As a result, he has almost replaced Custer in Grace's affections. Grace knew Jonathan was coming over tonight. She did her hair, put on her stockings and her best sandals. I could not tell if she was dressing up for Jonathan or for Mr. Sneff.

All I know is that Grace looked old. When grandmothers spend too much time on their hair, they look like old men with wigs on. Tonight her head was big as a marionette's and turned just as stiffly, as if someone were jerking strings behind the scenes. Her eyes were big and alert; she seemed to receive all the music through her pupils. "Skip to the last song on the second side!" she ordered Jonathan. "Marietta stole my album on account of this song."

> Each evening from December to December
> Before you drift to sleep upon your cot
> Think back to all the tales that you remember
> of Camelot.

Grace started crying as she listened to Richard Burton sing. "He was so handsome. And such a good actor."

"He was a drunk!" Lenore shouted from the kitchen. She emerged carrying a tray of Saltines and pepperoni.

"Let me hear the song!" Grace snapped. When it was over, she told Lenore to lay off the pepperoni. "You're getting fat," she said.

"And you're too old to be dating Mr. Sneff!" Lenore spat back.

Poison. Poison. Poison.

Grace got up to put the record needle on "What Do The Simple Folk Do?" Her sandals seemed to shuffle her around, their square two-inch heels offering a resolute finish to Grace's fragile ankles, around which her stockings had collected in soft nylon wrinkles.

Mr. Sneff arrived with another case of mineral water and stayed until Grace had played *Camelot* all the way through. The second time Richard Burton sang "Each evening from December to December," Grace got every bit as teary as the first. She turned to Mr. Sneff, and he reached for her hand behind the case of mineral water he had posed on the wicker desk.

I left the porch after "Camelot" because Mr. Sneff's cigar *stinks*, but especially because Grace and Mr. Sneff started talking about money. Mr. Sneff is a religious man whose faith requires more donations than most. Lately he has been quoting Jim Bakker —"If you pray for a camper, tell God what color," he said to Grace. When Jim and Tammy Faye needed money for a full-scale replica of the Old City of Jerusalem, he sent one hundred dollars. When they requested funds for a roller coaster that would tunnel riders through heaven and hell, he asked Grace for a contribution. Now that Heritage USA has gone bust, Mr. Sneff is looking for investments that are of interest to Grace. "Life's enough of a lottery," I heard her tell him. "If you want me, stick to real estate *here*, not in the hereafter."

Grace showed Mr. Sneff pictures of Marietta's condominium in Boca Raton, Florida. Then she started in on final wills and testaments. After that it was hospitals. And what about Bette, was she discharged from St. Vincent's? Did the insurance cover the price of the hip operation? They say she almost died! That sort of thing. Grace loves it. What she really loves is the fact that she is in good health and her peers are not. One reason Grace volunteers at the hospital is to see how well she is holding up against the other geriatrics. The other reason is her morbid curiosity. While Grace was on emergency room duty the other day, a nun was brought in because her vagina had collapsed out of disuse. Grace stayed with Sister Bonaventure until she was satisfied that she had been told the truth.

Jonathan challenged me to a Scrabble match, but I have temporarily lost my appetite for the game. Leo called to say he is arriving one week from today, on the eighteenth of August, and will spend two days with us before we go to Provincetown. Maria said he was looking for another job. She aimed her remarks at Lenore. "A headhunter called him about two job openings for September. He's already scheduled interviews."

I do not know what has lit a fire under Leo's normally sedentary rump. Mr. Welsh does not know Leo is joining us. So far the trip includes Custer and Carmencita, Maria and Leo, Mr. and Mrs. Welsh, Danny Dorino and his wife, Dottie, and Grace and me.

If Lenore knew that Maria was the focus of page after page of Mr. Welsh's amorous drivel, she would have kittens. Bad enough that Mr. Sneff has tried to invite himself to Provincetown. He is seventeen years younger than Grace, which in Lenore's eyes makes him an opportunist chasing an old widow.

Today's batch of letters from Mr. Welsh included a detailed chronology of his day, stapled to a fifteen-page account of Mr. Welsh's life. He enclosed press clips, baby pictures, army photographs, and his company's decal, NET GROWTH. On a smaller envelope, with a skull and crossbones drawn on it, Mr. Welsh had scribbled the words, Mothers for sodium pentothal. The letter inside held Mark Welsh's darkest secrets, many of which he had never told anyone. I will ask Maria if Mr. Welsh remembered to put how many ex-wives he has.

I did not open the letter that said Top Secret because I am sick of letters. But Monstro did. He was too restless to go to sleep, and came downstairs waving the envelope with the skull and crossbones on it. Maria's back was facing the staircase, so she did not see Monstro approach.

"Mommy, what's this?"

"You should be in bed!"

"Mommy, this has a skull on it!"

"It's not yours, it's none of your business," I said. I snatched it out of Monstro's hands. The quickness of my reflexes made him cry. I peeked inside while Maria comforted him.

"He's tired," Maria said, turning to thank me. "Come upstairs, Patrick. I'll read you *Robinson Crusoe*." She reached for his hand, but Monstro did not want to go. He twisted the top of his pajamas into a cotton corkscrew and dug his heels into our beige carpet.

I handed Maria the letter and left the living room to call Custer. I had not called him in weeks.

"What are you up to?"

"Reading."

"What?"

"Stuff I took out of the library."

"Grenada?"

"Yeah. How did you know?"

"Your girlfriend came over the other day."

"Oh. What for?"

"I don't know."

"You wanna come over?"

My heart beat faster. Custer usually came here. And he never asked me over.

"Where's your friend?"

"At a movie. I didn't wanna go."

"I'll be over in a few minutes. Gotta get rid of Jonathan first." I expected Custer to tease me about Jonathan, but he was remarkably subdued.

By the time I had made excuses to Jonathan, it was fairly late. I offered to walk him home and wished Grace, Mr. Sneff, Maria, Lenore, and Monstro good night.

Jonathan and I went out the back door. It was nine o'clock and a gash of crimson was the last bit of color in an otherwise charcoal sky. The pond was bursting with a pitch of activity that suggested rain. Crickets and frogs strained to out-rub and out-croak each other, and every able-bodied bird sang or shrieked a distinct melody—a bedlam of sopranos. Had I been able to sing, I would have joined in. The night demanded that kind of response.

Jonathan's reply was to feel omnipotent in love. Every song emboldened his toward actions he would usually never have considered. Ah, but if the birds are singing, or if a city skyline is particularly beautiful at twilight!—that is the way Jonathan reasons.

But here is where I am coming from. I expect a man in love to be capable of passion in less obvious settings. If Jonathan had tried to kiss me in the alley between our launderette and our superette, where danger and surprise fizz up the effort, then he would be the young man for me. As it stood, Jonathan did exactly what I expected. Before the screen door had even closed, he grabbed me by the back of my neck and tried to kiss me.

"Ouch!"

"I'm sorry."

"You're breaking my neck."

"Is that better?"

He relaxed his grip and held my face between his hands.

I shook my head out of the trap his palms had set for me.

"No. It's not."

Jonathan was hurt. I thought I would hear him whine like some abused puppy, but he was silent. I could feel him staring at me in the dark.

"You know what, Meredith?"

I did not answer.

"*I'm talking to you!*"

"What?"

"You're a pain in the ass! Do you hear me? I said, *You're a pain in the ass!* You know why? Because I can't do anything right. If I invite you on vacation, you turn around and accept another offer. Don't think I don't know you didn't invite me to the Cape! Everybody knows I'm not going and you didn't even bother to tell me. You're always waiting to see what else will come through! Yeah, well don't think I don't notice! And don't think I'm not pissed off! Just because I like you doesn't mean you're going to treat me like a dog! You're rude. Just plain rude! I don't even know why I persist in wanting to kiss a freckled redhead."

"I *don't* have freckles."

"You've got seven of them around your eyes. So shut up! Seven of them! And your father calls them the Pleiades. That's what you said and since I'm stupid enough to listen to you that's how I *know*. So shut up! You're a freckled redhead whether you like it or not and I don't even like redheads that much so maybe I'll get myself some good-looking blonde or brunette. Who needs redheads? I wouldn't kiss a redhead if my life depended on it!"

I had to smile.

"And damn it! I hate the way you smile or laugh when I'm upset. I think you've got a mean streak. I don't know how you got it, but you've got one all right. It runs down the middle of you like a groove." He drew a line from the sky to my head, and ran his index finger straight down my body—past my nose, my breasts, my navel, and even down to the part on the nun that had collapsed from disuse.

"Stop it!"

"With *pleasure*," he said firmly. "I have no interest in going any further."

That hurt.

As Jonathan turned to leave, I kicked him and collapsed his knee. He fell, then flipped on his stomach to grab my calf. He scrambled to his feet in a crouched position and, still holding my calf, squeezed it long and hard. I had to hop on my other foot to keep my balance.

"Don't *ever* do that again!" His voice was icy as our pond

water in winter. Even the frogs seemed to hush and listen.

He turned to go and I kicked him even harder.

This time Jonathan grabbed my shoulders and shoved me down on the grass. I tried to knee him, but he was too strong. "STOP IT, MEREDITH! I *mean* it!"

We must have wrestled for five minutes until I finally gave up and burst into tears. I was too proud to tell Jonathan what was bothering me. And he was wrapped up in his own anger and hurt. When he left me on the ground without saying a word, I was sure I had made an enemy for life.

By the time I reached Custer's, it was ten o'clock. He took one look at me and said I looked worse than a rooster after a cock fight. He applied witch hazel to the scrapes on my arms and legs and said I had the red stuff to look forward to as well.

"Not iodine!" I cried.

"No. Just Mercurochrome." His fingers were very gentle. "Who did this to you, Red?"

"It was *my* fault."

"Since when do you go pickin' fights with people stronger than you? You're too smart for that. I've never even known you to fight. Where'd all the testosterone come from?"

"I don't want to talk about it."

"What happened?"

I started crying. Lately, that is all I do. "Sorry," I sniffled. "Can't seem to stop crying."

"Last time I saw you cry it was because I had hurt your feelings—"

"I didn't cry!"

"True. Technically speaking, you did not cry. But when I saw you runnin' out back I knew you were going to. How else does that pond of yours stay full? We haven't had *that* much rain this summer."

I smiled.

"What happened?"

"I'm upset for the same reason I was mad at you."

Custer sighed, as if he did not have the energy to survive what he thought might be an attack. "You never told me why you were mad at me," he said.

"It was obvious—"

"You just stormed off and left me there to read your mind—"

"I'm very simple—"

"HA!" Custer laughed softly. "It's like unraveling the inside of a baseball."

"You're just thick, that's all." I smiled at Custer because I knew he was the only one strong enough to take me.

"I was upset—" I hesitated.

"Spit it out."

"I was upset because . . . You know what? I don't want to talk about me because you're not telling me what's bugging you."

"I'm fine. Don't weasel out of it."

I inspected Custer's face to see if he really was fine. He had his drawbridge up—nothing coming out—and would only open it for incoming remarks.

"I'll say it once and I want you to remember," I continued, "but then you've got to act as if I'd never said it." I looked at Custer and received his nod of agreement. "I was upset because sometimes I feel that I lost a lot of time when I was sick in ways that you and my other friends became more advanced." I looked down at my arms and legs, both stained with red patches.

"Is that what accounts for all this kicking and scratching?"

"I'm inexperienced."

"Did Jonathan pounce on you!"

"What does that have to do with—"

"Plenty! Look at these scratches. Did he try to do something you didn't want to do?"

"No."

"I don't believe you!"

It was hopeless. Custer got all wrapped up in the wrong scenario. The less subtle one. The one he could change by bashing Jonathan's face in the next time he saw him—yet I had already taken care of that! I tried several times to get Custer back to the issue of my sensitivity over my lack of experience. But he was determined to see me as the victim of Jonathan's aggression.

I tried to change the subject to Grenada, which Custer is usually eager to discuss. One of my questions finally bore through.

"What happened with that letter your mom gave you?"

"It was from a man who knew my father."

"That's *it?*"

"He sent a picture of himself with my dad in Barbados."

"Why Barbados?" Custer handed me the photograph.

"They launched part of the mission from Barbados."

Custer pointed to his father, who was getting into a helicopter. Officer Tomasino, the career officer who had sent it, was on the ground saluting Custer's father.

"That's a Blackhawk he's getting into. They use it to ferry Special Forces. They had C-130s for the Rangers, which is what my dad used to be. Lucky he wasn't jumping from five hundred feet like the Rangers in Grenada. First time U.S. troops had ever done that. See these helicopters?" Custer pointed to another picture Officer Tomasino had sent, "These are Marine HH-53s. A batch of students from the Grand Anse campus came out on these."

I was preoccupied with the photograph of Custer's father. All the features I had not been able to place when I interviewed Mrs. Welsh were apparent in her first husband—Custer was 50 percent his mother and 50 percent his father. The intelligence in his eyes came from his father.

Custer flipped through the *Operation Urgent Fury Report*, prepared by the Commander in Chief of the U.S. Atlantic Command (USCINCLANT). This was the *After-Action Report* I had glanced at the last time I was in his room. "Can't make anything out of this," Custer said, "it's all blacked out."

"How did you get it?"

"Miss Hart helped me do a Freedom of Information Act request."

He pointed to the map on the wall and traced a peninsula called Lance Aux Epines with his index finger. "Best I've been able to find out is that one Blackhawk crashed right here. But I don't know why my dad would have been in it. My dad was an officer, not a grunt. The officers stayed on the battleships or in Barbados."

"Who else have you been writing to?" Custer's obsession was slowly snapping me out of my discomfort over Jonathan.

"Officer Tomasino gave me some names. He said one medical student found a locket my father wanted me to have."

Custer pulled out an old *Time* magazine to show me pictures the medical students had taken of helicopters. While he was pointing to orange streaks, and explaining about antiaircraft fire from 23 millimeter double-barreled ZU guns, two big tears escaped my hands and landed on the orange part of the photo.

"What's the matter now?" Custer said.

"The l-l-l-locket," I sputtered.

Custer looked very sad, much older, and had a tenderness in his eyes that brought more tears to mine. "Oh, forget about it," he said. "Probably just his dog tag."

Custer stood up and went over to his desk. I waited a bit, then followed him. My impulse was to put my arms around him, however foreign this behavior was to us, but when I got to the desk I noticed he was at the point where pain is so utter, the kindest thing is *not* to intrude.

We stood alongside each other for about a minute. Custer toyed with Officer Tomasino's letter on his desk, picking it up and dropping it with the slow rhythms of a church bell.

I waited for—what is for me—a very long time. About thirty seconds. Then I erupted.

"Goddamn it, Custer!—what's the matter?"

He handed me the letter he had been playing with.

I was confused. "Something in here?"

"Read it."

I was frightened. "You tell me," I whispered. I handed the letter back. I surveyed the Mercurochrome battlefield on my legs for a second time, looked up, and told Custer point-blank that if he did not tell me what was bothering him I would terminate our friendship.

Custer smiled weakly, and when those muscles collapsed —something stiff and pained took over around his eyes and mouth. Finally, he spoke.

"I lied to you, Red. I got a letter all right, but it didn't say what I told you."

Custer picked up the photographs and blinked so rapidly it was not long before I realized he was trying to hold back tears. Custer never cries. The only other time I have seen him in tears is when I am—or he *thinks* I am—sick.

"My father didn't die in battle," he said.

I waited. And waited some more.

"He shot himself in the head after he found out my mother had remarried."

Nothing could have prepared me for this statement. I sat on Custer's bed and watched him stare at the photographs. When I had finally registered what Custer said, I was confused. "But he's in the pictures," I protested feebly.

"He was in Grenada, but—"

"But what?"

"The officer who wrote me said he turned to his commanding officer and said—"

"Said what?"

"He turned to his commanding officer and said—"

"Said *what?*"

Custer could not finish. He broke down, choking on his own grief, and covered his face with his large, strong hands. After sobbing for what seemed like half an hour, my poor friend was exhausted. I vowed I would never ask another question that had to do with his father, and just as I was about to give up on the statement he had never finished, I heard Custer mumble from behind his hands.

"He said to his commander, 'For the sake of my kid, make sure the report reads Dead in Combat.'" Custer took in a short gasp of air, and continued. "Then he held a pistol to his temple and blew his brains out."

I closed my eyes and quickly opened them because all I could see under my lids was blood. Outside, the storm noises were coming up—birds, frogs, and crickets. I sat on the bed, and after a silence that took us through several cycles of the mockingbird's song, I said, "That officer never should have told you the truth."

"It's not his fault."

"What did you say his name was?"

"Tomasino. Officer Tomasino."

"Tom Asshole Sino. He never should have written that letter." I was so upset, I felt if the man had been in the room I would have beaten him with my own two fists.

"I would have wanted to know, eventually." The life was sucked out of Custer's voice.

"Where's he buried?" I asked. It came out like a whisper.

"Down there."

"Grenada?"

"On a hill near the Point Salines airport."

"Why didn't they bury him in the U.S.?"

"Don't know."

"Can't hear you."

"I SAID I DON'T KNOW!"

I started to cry. Custer never yelled at me. And I always cry when I am yelled at. When he saw me hiding my eyes behind my right palm, he pulled my hand away and said he was sorry.

"My dad left instructions not to contact his relatives. He just referred to his will." Custer sighed, and continued in a low, flat voice. "From the sound of it, he'd been planning the suicide for a while, and was just waiting around for a combat mission to disguise it."

Custer was beat. I asked if he would like to be by himself, and he immediately exclaimed, "No! Stay with me, Red." He talked a bit about his grandmother Annie Fourchette, who is coming up from Mississippi with Buster.

"Who's Buster?" I said.

"Her dog."

"Just what we need."

"Grandma Fourchette is a great old lady."

"No—the dog. The last thing we need around here is another dog."

My mind hopped back to Custer's father.

"Custer?"

"What?"

"Why didn't they give your dad an army burial?"

Custer struggled with his feelings, then he calmed down and replied, "I think suicide is an automatic dishonorable discharge. And you don't get an army burial if you've been discharged."

"Didn't the commanding officer respect his final wishes?"

"The commanding officer did. Tomasino leaked it. That's why he wrote me."

"What do you mean?"

"He said he'd go to his grave feeling guilty about what he'd done. Doesn't even know why he told his superiors. Stress of first combat, he said."

"Asshole!"

"No—really Red, they say it happens."

"Bullshit."

"Do you want to read his letter?"

"NO. I'm sick and tired of letters—the ones I've seen lately come from sadists or crazies!"

"Poor guy sent me a check from his first steady job, he felt so bad."

"Poor guy! How can you say that?" I calmed down for Custer's sake. "How much?"

"What?"

"The check."

"Five hundred dollars."

Not even enough to pay for a decent burial, I thought.

"Is it true about the locket?"

"Yeah—Tomasino tracked down the student and it's on the way."

Custer turned once again to the photographs, and looked at each one very slowly.

"You were closer to your dad than you let on."

"I guess. Tough to say—" Custer looked up. "A father is a father. Particularly if you don't have one."

I suddenly thought of my parents, and my eyes started acting up again.

"Forget about it, Red," Custer said quietly. "Maybe we'd have hated each other by now—"

"B-b-b-ut yo-o-o-o-u'll n-n-n-ever have a ch-ch-ch-ance to find out!"

These outbursts were becoming an embarrassment, and they certainly did not help Custer. I quickly squashed my emotions and, as matter-of-factly as possible, said, "Custer, you can have my dad. We'll share him. He cares about you."

"You got a good one."

"Don't you like my mother?"

"YES, I like your mother. Jesus, you're so defensive! We were talking about fathers."

I smiled. "You've got a good mom, too," I offered. "Does she know what happened to your dad?"

"If she does, she doesn't let on. She didn't read Tomasino's letter—just passed it on to me. But I think she must know because she asked me if I wanted to see a psychiatrist."

"Do you want to?"

"I want to talk to *her*. But it's awful hard talking to someone who wants to pretend it never happened." Custer sounded frustrated. He added, "She's a little distracted lately."

I stopped myself from telling Custer about Mr. Welsh and Maria. He had enough problems.

Custer turned toward the window.

"What?" I asked.

"Thought I heard a car."

I stood up and looked out. Custer's parents were driving down Highland. Mr. Welsh's car slowed down to a full stop in front of our house. No lights on our porch. All lights out.

"Yikes! It's your parents. Call you tomorrow—" As I ran out, Custer grabbed me by the arm and pulled me toward him to say, "Thanks, Red." He squeezed me so hard my breasts smashed up against his chest, and ached thereafter.

I sneaked out the back door and heard Rufus-Coco barking his lungs off. Then Lafayette joined in. The rain had started, making our pachysandras slippery as wet rubber. When I fell, Lafayette barked louder in sympathy. The thunder started up as I slipped through our back door. I could barely make out a conversation on the front porch. The porch light was on. I saw Mr. Welsh. Maria whispered, "What are you doing here?"

"I had to see you, Saunders." He smiled sheepishly.

"Yeah, well, beat it! You can't come over here. Go on—before somebody sees you."

She turned off the light. Mr. Welsh kept talking.

"Custer's asleep. I told Louisa I was going for a walk."

"In the rain?"

"That didn't surprise her."

For about one minute I could not hear a thing. My heart was thumping. The thunder was rolling hard. In the clear spots between noises, I was troubled by the absence of conversation. Only steamy silences and the rain tapping the leaves on our sugar maple.

Finally, I heard Mr. Welsh say, "I love you, Saunders. I really do." He said it very softly, as if he had just kissed Maria.

"You're married," she replied. She said it very softly, as if she had just surrendered.

"I can fix that," he said.

A flash of lightning lit up Maria's white nightgown. In the same instant, I could see Mr. Welsh standing below her, on the first porch step. He was wet, and Maria's upper body, which was folded over him, looked like a sleek white seal resting comfortably on his shoulder.

Then it was dark again.

Another flash of lightning and I saw that Mr. Welsh had come up a step. He was still holding Maria. And I think her arms were around his waist.

He was murmuring, "One mississippi, two mississippi—"

The thunder sounded.

"That was two miles away," Maria said.

I waited through several cycles of light and thunder. Each time, Mr. Welsh counted the *mississippis*, and Maria estimated the miles.

"If you're so good at counting," she said in a quiet, steady voice, "why don't you tell me how many times you've been married."

"It's all in the letter, Maria. I swear it is. Everything I hate myself for is in there. But there's one thing I'm sure of—"

"Yes. I know. And haven't you been sure of that before?"

"Not like this. Never like this."

When his voice broke, I felt like a ten-year-old listening to an opera tenor: I did not know whether to laugh or cry.

I almost felt sorry for Mr. Welsh when Maria said, "You can't come over here like this. If you ever become available, then and only then *might* I take this whole thing seriously."

"I will, Saunders," he said. "Mark my words, I *will*."

It was quiet for a very long time. The night belonged to the dogs, the birds, the rain, and the thunder. Part of it belonged to Maria and Mr. Welsh. But most of it belonged to Custer.

14.

One Virgin's Opinion and Louisa Welsh's Secret

Maria did not exactly lie about Leo. She just massaged the truth. This way and that, she has been rubbing the facts for the past few days. Not until this morning did she tell us Leo had been fired.

After seven years at Thomas & Morris, Leo was told that his management of the Tasti-Whip account had cost him his job. A senior manager from Tasti-Whip, a long-standing client of Thomas & Morris, wrote a memo to Leo's boss describing Mr. Malcolm's attitude. "A supercilious disregard for the gravity of Tasti-Whip's million-dollar midair disaster characterizes much of the spirit and the substance of the consultant's work." No name was mentioned, but everyone knew who it was. This came as a surprise to the people at Thomas & Morris, where Leo was highly respected for the quality and consistency of his work. But yesterday, Leo was asked to leave. He had one hour to collect most of his belongings while a security guard watched his every move. The measures were particularly harsh because Thomas & Morris had heard that Leo was being headhunted by their major competitor. They wanted to make sure none of Leo's files left the office.

"Security breach," Leo had told Maria. He claimed he did

not know how, when, or why, but someone had tipped Thomas & Morris off about his job hunt. As for the letter from Tasti-Whip, he had no clue as to why it had happened, and said the charges were totally unfounded.

The facelessness of the operation was breathtaking. At no time was Leo allowed to speak with his superiors. The same applied for the colleagues he had played softball with on the company team. Within twenty-four hours of his dismissal, photographs of Leo were posted throughout the company, with the words REPORT THIS MAN TO SECURITY written underneath.

Last night Maria had sought Mr. Welsh's advice on the matter. "Those big firms chew you up and spit you out," he had said. "I'm sorry for your friend." He did not know which friend.

Today I joined Maria outside. I wanted to talk about Custer's father, but it felt very wrong. If Custer had hesitated to tell me, I doubt he would want anyone else to know.

I have been trying to reach Custer all morning; his mother said he had gone for a run. Maria has Leo on the brain, so the path of least resistance suggested that a polite comment on Leo's misfortunes was easy and appropriate.

"I can't believe it," I said, "Leo's the kind of guy who never gets fired."

"Anybody can get fired. Lenore's ass-kisser theory was wrong. Leo's independence cost him his job."

"How's that? Leo doesn't strike me as the kind of man who makes waves. I agree with Leo. Sounds like somebody squealed on him."

"I think you're both wrong about him."

Maria was sunning herself on the lawn. Lafayette was jumping in and out of our pond, looking for anything she could clamp between her jaws. Lenore had taken Elizabeth and Monstro to camp, and Grace was inside listening to *Camelot* for the eight hundredth time.

"I wish Mom and Dad were back," I said.

"Do you miss them?"

"Things would not be so crazy."

"What do you mean?"

I sneezed. The pollen count was unusually high. After I had blown my nose, I thought about the least intrusive way to bring up what I had seen last night. I watched Lafayette pull something out of the pond. "Ugh. She'll dredge up anything," Maria said. Lafayette dragged a soggy clump of paper and leaves toward Rufus-Coco.

"I saw you last night," I said. Maria waited for me to continue. "And I guess my question is: if you care about Leo, how could you let Mr. Welsh approach you like that?"

Maria was startled by the directness of my inquiry—and so was I.

"It's not that simple," she said.

"What do mean it's not that simple?"

"Just what I said."

"Well, which one do you want?"

My question, I thought, would help Maria focus.

"He's married, Meredith. It's not a matter of choosing."

"Then why did you let him kiss you last night?"

"I don't know. He understands me. He's very wise and passionate. And I respect him the more I hear him do the show."

"For what?"

"For the same reasons you've said you respect him. He's

smart, he's involved, we've got the same sense of humor, and I like the answers he gives to the audience. He's a maverick—"

"Augh!—I *hate* that word! He always uses it. Everybody's a maverick in business. There can't be that many mavericks in the world."

"You know what I mean. When he broke out on his own, he didn't have a dime. You've got to respect a man who left a six-figure income and started his own company. I have yet to pull off that sound system I've been talking about, so I admire anyone who succeeds that way. And with all the pressures on him, he's been very thoughtful."

"I think he loves you. That's why I asked you which one you wanted."

"And I answered that he was married."

"Knowing him, he'll get unmarried. He and Louisa were both married when they met."

"She's a nice woman."

"Yeah, she's not so bad. She said something very beautiful when I interviewed her for *The Chronicle*."

"Do I want to hear this?"

"I don't think it will bother you. She said that ballerinas these days are too concerned about executing the thirty-two *fouettés* in *Swan Lake* without falling. And that's not the point. Technique, yes, she said. But what is lacking, which the Russians have in abundance, she claimed, is the boldness or individuality of interpreting the roles. That's what makes every *Giselle* different."

"Well, if she said that, we really can't fault Mr. Welsh for his taste in women, can we?"

Maria could be extraordinarily gracious at the very moments

most people become small-minded. She could also be very tough on me. When I suggested that she think seriously about her situation, she grew irritated. I was speaking very slowly, choosing my words carefully in order to avoid offending her, when, finally, she interrupted.

"Oh, really? Tell me about it. Does something in your experience address my situation?"

I did not take it personally.

"This is one situation you don't have to live through to know about," I said. "Besides, I feel somewhat responsible for getting you and Leo together—and if you need to talk to someone more *experienced*, there's always Lenore."

"Don't get me started on Lenore. She's been twisted since John left her."

"She left him."

"That's a lie. He left her. And Lenore doesn't want anyone to know."

"What really happened?"

"He chose booze over her. They usually do."

"Do you think your problem is as serious?"

"No."

"It's pretty bad, though. Mark Welsh is after you. And he's not going to quit until he gets you. If he makes himself available, what'll you do?"

"Meredith—" she had that you're-repeating-yourself voice on—"that's a big if."

"But what if he does?"

"I'll think about it when he does."

"What will you say to Leo?"

"Nothing."

"Nothing?"

"That's what I said. Lenore can't stand him anyway."

We both smiled.

"Yeah, well she'll take Leo over Mr. Welsh any day!"

"Which one do you like, Meredith?"

To my surprise, I had no trouble answering. "Neither one," I said. "Leo needs more Mark Welsh in him. And Mark Welsh needs more Leo in him. When we're in Provincetown, maybe they'll collide over you and become the same person."

The phone rang. From outside, it sounded like a silver ribbon wafting toward our ears. After four rings, we concluded that Grace had gone upstairs into the air-conditioning and could not hear it.

Louisa Welsh was on the other end. She sounded businesslike, but not in the confident way I expected. "Is Maria there?" she asked. I said she was. "Tell her I'll be right over, Meredith."

Within ten minutes, Louisa Welsh was standing on the same step her husband had stood on the night before. Lafayette was licking Mrs. Welsh's ankles, and when I looked farther north I noticed she was holding a wet envelope in one hand and the letter she had removed from it in the other.

She asked to speak to Maria.

"You just missed her," I said. I recognized the letter as the one I had tried to burn and drown. Thanks a lot, Lafayette, I muttered to myself. Next time I will let that yellow jacket take a good sharp nip.

"Meredith, I wish you had told her to wait."

"I did," I insisted, "but her boyfriend called from the train station."

"Her boyfriend?"

"Yes, Leo Malcolm," I said, knowing full well he was not due for another six days. "He's coming with us to Provincetown. Grace and I are the only guests without boyfriends." I let the information sink in. "Actually," I added, "even Grace has a boyfriend, but I don't think he's coming." Then I asked, "How are you today, Mrs. Welsh?"

She looked down at the letter she was pinching between the thumb and index finger of her left hand. The pages had dried and the ballpoint letters reminded me of the veins on my grandmother's wrists, Bic Medium blue under onionskin.

I saw that Mrs. Welsh wanted desperately to talk to someone and it was painful to watch.

"Were you happy with the article I wrote about you?"

Two large tears rolled unevenly down her cheeks. She wiped them quickly and said, "Yes, Meredith. Very much so. Yes. It was lovely."

I had no stomach for further deception. Instinct had made me protect Maria, but I am convinced she is not blameless.

After Mrs. Welsh turned to leave, I ran out back, grabbed Maria's arm, silenced her before she could say anything, and pulled her inside.

"She knows," I said. I felt sick.

"What are you talking about?"

"Mrs. Welsh," I repeated. "She *knows*."

Howdoesheknow? What wereyoudoingreadingmyletterandburningitinthefirstplace? Goddamnthatdog! All followed in spitfire succession.

After the explanations were in, Maria was angry with me. She claimed she was not hiding anything from me and that even if she were it would be her right. Last night's visit was as much a surprise to her as it was to me, she said.

"You didn't have to kiss him," I said.

"I feel very comfortable with him."

"But you didn't have to kiss him."

"You're right. I didn't have to kiss him."

"You wanted to."

Maria looked me over, scanning my face as if she suddenly questioned the trustworthiness of our blood knot. Finally she said, "I wanted to."

This admission threw me into a slate of confusion more massive than Maria's. I love my sister. I admire my sister. And it is possible I am judging too quickly. But shouldn't Maria know that Mr. Welsh is off limits? Then I wondered why Louisa had left George V. Daniels for Mark Welsh. To me, this seemed inconceivable.

"Was he fat then?" I had once asked Custer.

"That's sometimes not an issue, Red."

"Why would a woman leave a thin man in an officer's uniform for a fat man who yells a lot and hates wearing suits?"

"She loves him."

"Because he's a millionaire?"

"No. I really think she loves him."

"Am I missing something?"

"Before she got married, my mother introduced Mark Welsh to me as a brilliant, tender, thoughtful man who loved her, and who understood her completely. All the things we never see."

I remembered this conversation as I talked to Maria.

"What is it about him?" I asked.

"I think he loves me."

"So what."

Maria did not want to talk about it anymore. I pushed too hard until finally she said, "I appreciate your concern, Meredith. I really do. And I respect your experience in matters that have made you very wise for your age. But in other areas, your knowledge is a bit too virginal."

Too virginal. Here we go again.

Leo is arriving in six days, Mrs. Welsh has just found out about her husband. We have no guarantee that she will keep silent with either Mr. Welsh or Custer. In eight days we leave for vacation. And I am being too virginal.

I know what Lenore would say. But I cannot speak with Lenore. I cannot admit to Mrs. Welsh that I know. I have to pretend that everything is A-okay with Mr. Welsh. And I must not tell Grace.

I cannot even talk to Custer.

Who can I talk to? Carmencita? The woman who has just confessed her undying love for the man who is madly in love with my sister?

This never would have happened if my parents had stayed home.

15.

Carmencita's Problem

Goddamn her. Carmencita's in trouble. Big trouble. She called in tears yesterday and said she needed to talk to me. Her whole system was so choked up I could not make out a word. At first I thought she had somehow found out that Mr. Welsh was in love with Maria or that Custer's father had committed suicide. But no. She was babbling about Saint Agatha.

"What's this about Saint Agatha?" I asked when Carmencita arrived at the door of our porch.

She burst into more tears and looked so awful I finally yelled, "Stop that! Whatever it is, it can't be that bad."

Between Carmencita's sighs and hiccups, I made out that her parents had raised her on the story of Saint Agatha. The Roman prefect Quintianus had chased after Agatha. But so chaste and devout was Agatha that she rejected his advances and endured the tortures he inflicted on her. Her emblem is the breast because she cut hers off rather than succumb to Quintianus.

"That's ridiculous," I said. "She should have given in. *Nobody* these days would do that. It's a dumb story, even if it comes from your parents."

"They're very religious."

"That's not religion. That's slaughter. Is that what's bothering you?"

My question provoked another eyeburst. I lost my patience.

"Go upstairs and wash that makeup off!" I ordered. "How can you have a good cry when you've got goop all over your face?" Big glops of water had smeared her face with mascara and eyeshadow. Underneath, her cheeks were red with heat.

My remark triggered more tears. I suddenly felt sorry for Carmencita and went over to give her a hug. She buried her face against my breast pocket with such shame and intensity I worried that the button would mark her face permanently. After about three minutes holding her body wracked with sighs and sobs, I heard her talk to my button. "Carmencita, I can't hear you," I said softly. "Please speak up."

The wailing started all over again. "I skipped my period," she said. She would not raise her head.

"How late are you?"

"Two months."

"Two months!" My shock produced more anxiety. "Did you tell Custer?"

"No."

"Are you going to?"

She wiped her eyes, looked up at me, and said. "You're the only person I can talk to."

The sickly weight of Carmencita's dependence overtook me like a bad fume. Still, I was glad Custer had not been told yet; the news would put him into a complete tailspin.

"What are you going to do?"

She ungummed herself from me, stood up, and collapsed into the wicker chair opposite mine. "I don't know," she said.

"Didn't you use rubbers?"

"No."

"Why?"

"Custer said they're like taking a shower with your socks on."

"He did?"

"Yes. He called them raincoats."

"That's totally irresponsible of him."

"So I used a diaphragm. But I guess it happened the one time I didn't bother to put it in."

We were lost in our own thoughts for a while.

"I can't believe Custer refused to wear a raincoat. Never mind the pregnancy stuff, but with all the viruses crawling around—"

"We weren't sleeping with other people."

"Still."

I changed the subject. "So what will you do?"

"I *told* you! I don't know."

"Sorry."

"That's okay." Carmencita tried to smile. "You know how religious my parents are."

"I know." I noticed that Carmencita had started wearing a cross around her neck. "But if you need to see a doctor, I'll go with you."

16.

A Digression on the Nature of Life

After Carmencita left, I was very depressed. I cannot remember when I had thought so much about serious things. My illness, maybe. Custer's news about his father triggered it. Last night I had horrible nightmares. Maria pregnant with Mr. Welsh's child. Lenore aborting her own two children. My brother being born again. And me giving birth to a little girl who looked like me during chemotherapy. I woke up moaning and Lenore came immediately. I woke up a second time. This time Maria came in. "Did he make you pregnant?" I asked. Who? "Mr. Welsh." Maria stayed with me until I calmed down. As I drifted off to sleep, I could hear Lenore and Maria whispering in my room. They were worried that I was dreaming about death again. I wanted to tell them that my dreams had always been peaceful on that subject, but I was caught in their web of swollen whispers, which lulled me off to sleep. I wanted to tell them not to worry about me. Don't call Mom and Dad, I said. But the words never escaped. These are just nightmares, I wanted to say. But I could not crack sleep's membrane. For the next few hours, my dreams were far more terrifying than any I had ever experienced when I was sick.

My restless night resulted in today's worthlessness. Fatigue has rendered me useless for anything but thought. I have no influence over the day and feel as if I am underwater, with shadows rippling and changing above me, suggesting more energetic lives. People go about their business while I am not participating.

I thought about Carmencita's dilemma, reflecting first on the nature of religion. Grace's favorite story is about the death of Saint Ursula and her ten thousand virgins at the hand of German infidels.

For most people religion is the discipline they would otherwise not have—a church mural in which the eyes always seem to be following them. My parents did not raise me in any particular faith, but I consider myself religious. For me, religion has nothing to do with Saint Agatha or Saint Ursula. When someone has a presence more enduring than the time you have actually spent with them, that is what I call life; that is the only definition of mystery and faith that seems to me worth cultivating. That is why I am sure my parents still have conversations with the son they lost. It is also why I am certain Custer is in knots about his father's death. In general, whatever moves people to love should carry them to a place more spiritual than that of their daily existence.

On the surface, Lenore is the least spiritual in our family. She will say things like, "You can't even eat shrimp without noticing that shitty little string that runs through it." But I do not read her on this level. A lot more is going on. Maria is having trouble finding people she can connect with on this unspoken level. Physical love is not the way to do it, she says, though she claims she once cried after making love because she was convinced the man, she would not say who, had broken through to her soul. Maria says her generation has pedestrian concerns. People couple and uncouple. They are not living the lives they expected to lead. An adhesive is missing. Once they had been young and sweet, but life had got them when their hearts could be broken and stomped out any tenderness. A lot of people are living alone, adjacent to each other, the smallest unit being oneself. Maria said it was not very satisfying, but at least it did not hurt.

Custer has suffered enough to have a soul. Grace has not suffered in ways that have caused her to develop this intangible necessity. Her commitment to life is more material. My grandmother is fully aware another world exists, but she is not interested in becoming a member. Practical concerns consume her, which is why she and Mr. Sneff get along. She has already paid for her plot in the Mainsfield cemetery five blocks away—"That way, I'll be able to walk," she says.

Most people I know are capable of seeing beyond the demands of daily life. It is just a matter of whether they choose to value it. I think the reason I admire my parents so much is that, with everything they have been through, they manage to make life seem worthwhile.

I asked Custer whether he envied people who went through life without wrestling as much. He said, "Envy? No. Why waste your time with those people?" But I do envy them. I envy Leo, for instance, and the way he moves through life like a minnow, changing direction unthinkingly as millions change with him. I sometimes wish life's process could be a bit more like coloring my mother's hair. The plastic gloves you peel off the instruction sheet protect your hands from the chemicals, and in the end my mother looks more beautiful—at least I think so. So why is it that we have been given neither instructions nor membrane to protect us from the moleculars of day-to-day encounters with humans? When we achieve an inner beauty, we have generally suffered for it.

Custer was telling me how in the military KISS means Keep It Simple Stupid. The principle never works for civilian life. And maybe that is the difference. When I am honest with myself, I admit that civilians like me do not seem to be able to keep anything simple—sometimes because life will not let me, as in the case of my leukemia, and other times because I choose to complicate my existence. Some people can stare at the PENALTY OF LAW sticker on a pillow and wonder what would happen to them if they ripped it off. Me, I want to rip it off and see if the sirens come to take me away. I will not wait for the universe to explode. I want it exploding all around me. So when people talk of the destruction of the universe, which will happen eventually, the matter of when being the only issue, I ask myself: Why should our age be riper than any other? Why have doomsayers always predicted apocalypses in their lifetime? Are they worried they might miss it?

If we are to be conserved in particles afterwards, I want every one of mine to be charged. Even if it means exhausting myself while I am here. I will visit the grave of Custer's father even if it makes us sad for days. In the same way that Lenore's husband uses cocktails to extend the spell of the day, I will go to whatever lengths to intoxicate myself. Sometimes this causes me to look into the sky at night and mistake a plane for a shooting star. Or when fireworks rain from the sky like sea urchins, I know I am staring into the heart of our glittering universe. The pop of combat, a burst of ruby chrysanthemums, and the shimmering tails of dying light are all I need for proof.

I know most people are content with a lot less. But I am not just concerning myself with massive things. I am talking about Elizabeth's resourcefulness last Halloween—when she stuck wires in her braids, headdress like a caribou. I am referring to the way Lenore wraps each sock separately at Christmas to stretch the quantity of her feelings about us, even if she has no money. I am pointing out how Grace hangs in our existence like an inchworm—vulnerable and expectant—yet tough enough to hook herself onto the next perch after we have cut her down. And I am remembering something perfectly simple, yet no less capable of turning my heart inside out: The way Custer looked at me the night he told me about his father.

I am suggesting that our job is to shake things up while we are here.

Whatever the consequences.

Part Three

The Dunes of Provincetown

I ate the day
Deliberately, that its tang
Might quicken me all into verb, pure verb.

—Seamus Heaney, "Oysters"

17. The Road to Provincetown

I am sorry for Mrs. Welsh, but I would crawl on my belly through malarial swamps if I knew it would make her suffer in silence. I want this vacation, I need this vacation, and I will not be surprised if my source of pleasure becomes Louisa Welsh's source of pain. The workings of the heart are familiar to anyone who has visited the Franklin Museum in Philadelphia. I was ten years old when I got lost inside the massive corridors of the inferior vena cava. For thirty minutes I wandered—frightened—and finally emerged chastened by tremendous knowledge: the heart would be the source of all turbulence for myself and others.

By the end of the day, we will be in Provincetown. Leo arrived the day before yesterday, polite as ever, and acting as if he had never been fired. We did not have room for him in our house. The Mainsfield Motor Inn put him up, so he has been a comfortable mile away from the Alphabet Streets. Yesterday he joined us for a barbecue. He was the only one among us who knew how to use the propane grill. He even gave us a history of the canisters used to store the fuel. Gumbey Metals had once been a client of his and Leo was called upon to help determine which colors sold better than others.

(Our propane canister is rust. Not rust color, just rust. Originally it was cake-batter yellow, but it has been made uniformly rusty by the elements and Grace once mistook the whole contraption for a planter.)

Leo described Gumbey's assembly line, how they used top-grade steel, and how a guy by the name of Mark Welsh, a consultant to Thomas & Morris at the time, got spray-painted at the point they were coloring the canisters pink—an experiment to make the propane grills less frightening to women. "I tried to protect him," Leo explained. "He was my superior. But he was so inquisitive and got so excited he ran right through the assembly line to the pay phone in the factory. He said he had to call his girlfriend."

Four pairs of ears—Maria's, Lenore's, Grace's, and mine—were perked up high as Lafayette's. Grace was about to ask a question, but Leo went on with his story.

"He asked her if she would use a pink propane grill. She said she didn't care what color it was, she was more concerned about the fact that when it exploded it would take her and the house with it. Who cares whether it's pink or blue when it does *that*, she said.

"Welsh came back to tell the client the results of his 'research' and Gumbey was so impressed they redesigned their sales efforts around education rather than color. 'Teach the customer to use the thing, *then* play with colors,' Welsh said. 'Otherwise it's a lie you can't live down.' So there I was watching my boss, spray-painted pink, being taken seriously by Gumbey. I had to hand it to the guy. He was a crazy, but had lots of flair."

"What happened to his girlfriend?" Maria asked feebly.

"He married her eventually. He brought her along on a

Thomas & Morris outing and she performed the dying swan from *Swan Lake*—dressed like a pink propane drum with a tutu. Welsh told us she used to dance with Balanchine."

"Louisa *did* dance with Balanchine!" Grace piped up.

We were all uncomfortably silent. Except Grace. And Leo looked confused. He asked Grace how she knew Mrs. Welsh.

Just as Grace was about to answer, Maria interrupted. "We don't know her well," she said. "None of us knows her very well—"

"But she'll be going to Provincetown with you," Lenore added. "Along with her husband."

Leo's politeness was showing signs of strain.

"He's such a nice man," Grace gushed, "He inscribed my copy of his book—"

"*Mergers in America*?"

"That's right."

Lenore cut Grace off to finish. "He rented the house on the dunes and invited all the business show employees."

Leo glanced at Maria, and she anticipated his question.

"Didn't I tell you other people were coming?" she asked.

"Of course you did, I just didn't know who the people were."

Leo had his Chief of Protocol voice on. I would have respected him more if he had gotten obsessive at that moment, asking us how we knew Mr. Welsh, why he was coming, and how this whole thing had started. Instead he kept the propane grill going. When he closed the cover of the grill, it was my way of knowing the information had disturbed him.

"Isn't that dangerous?" I asked.

"What?"

"To put the lid on. Couldn't it explode?"

"You're right," he said.

"Do you ever explode?" I asked, my voice calming to a whisper so the others would not hear.

"Pardon?"

"I said," still whispering, "do you ever pop, yell, display your temper—that sort of thing."

"Meredith, this conversation is hardly appropriate." He gave an unnecessary amount of attention to the hamburgers, which were not even close to being ready.

"I introduced you to my sister," I challenged. The banality of Leo's politeness seemed less *appropriate* under the circumstances. I felt like saying: Admit it!—You can't stand Mark Welsh and you're pissed off he's coming on vacation with us. Instead I asked, "Is Mr. Welsh still working with your company?"

"Very much so. He's on the board and is a consultant on retainer."

"What does that mean?"

"It means that he doesn't work with us on a daily basis. He works out of his own office and gets paid when he consults."

Leo brushed each burger with cocktail sauce.

"Does he live near here?" he asked.

"See that castle over there?" I pointed toward the red granite tower.

Leo looked up, and I saw his marble eyes jiggle a little in their sockets.

"He's our neighbor," I said.

I turned toward the others, half-hoping Maria had heard our discussion. But she had gone inside. Lenore was trying to keep Elizabeth from killing Monstro with our hamburger spatula. Grace had gone to retrieve her inscribed copy of *Mergers in America*. And Leo did not ask any more questions.

After provoking someone who responds in such a puny fashion, I felt like running up a tree or doing fifty push-ups to put my combat energy elsewhere. I asked myself why Leo bugs me so much, and, never reaching a conclusion, I continued to stare at Leo's perfectly ordinary face. I decided that he should lose his hair. Go bald, maybe. Then he would suffer. Then he might change fundamentally. Men who have had hair and lost it become less smug. Make more of an effort. Their lack of confidence turns them into extroverts in the best sense.

18.

The Cartwheel

Provincetown. We made it. Two cars loaded down with beach paraphernalia, which we transferred onto jeeps. Then we let some of the air out of our tires and drove east until we almost fell into the ocean.

Nobody here but us Mainsfielders. Beauty has overcome all anguish. Personal vendettas are being silenced by a roaring surf, and the niggling little tensions that adhere to us are less a concern than the tar which now sticks to the bottom of our feet.

The Atlantic is ice-cold, even in August. Grace got as far as her ankles and called for help, saying she could not move. Leo went to her rescue. His long white body looked smooth and vulnerable out of clothes.

Mr. Welsh's body merits some discussion. Have you ever seen the After pictures when little boys have successfully reduced in Fat Boy camps? They are less bulky, no question, but they still look fatter than most people, and you can always tell that they used to be fat because their skin hangs in flat pockets where there used to be purses of blubber. Mr. Welsh's skin has a little more tone because he has been exercising while trimming down. Also, his active personality and handsome face make you concentrate on his good looks and energy rather than his profile. But when he sits down there is still evidence of the dirigible that used to be there.

Carmencita would not care if the *Hindenburg* were permanently affixed to Mr. Welsh's body. She looks at him as if he were her only hope for escape from her current problem. I should add that Carmencita, because she is part witch, managed to buy the same cheetah bathing suit as me. At two months she is not showing, and the only reason she decided to come on this trip was to buy time—to figure out what to do about the little person growing inside her.

Carmencita and I recognize the gravity of the situation, but sometimes we invent ways of talking about it that make her smile. We have a code name for the person. We call it C-squared because it represents the multiplication of Custer and Carmencita. When I am by myself, I sometimes have difficulty being amused. One of the side effects of chemotherapy is sterility, so Carmencita's situation makes me wonder if I will ever be able to have children.

I did not expect the sand to be so grainy out here. But this is not some tame beach with lifeguards and sand smooth as confectioner's sugar. This is a real beach, the savage kind. Big shells make granular shell-meal, and the surf can scrape you in its most aggressive postures. The undertow is a force we have quickly come to respect.

Carmencita was the first one in, but she ended up being the most frightened. Her confidence was met with a smack of waves more certain and constant than any power she has ever known. I watched Carmencita struggle with every step, sea foam riding up her legs until the spots on her bathing suit disappeared.

Custer ran after her, and when Carmencita emerged, her shiny black hair was coiled like rope around her neck. She was shaking, goose-bumped, and slick with tanning oil that showed off her muscle tone. Her eyes were huge, black, and terrified. But as she recovered her legs, wobbly and stiff with cold, and gained control of her face, twisted with fright, I could see her looking toward Mr. Welsh, evaluating the sympathy of his response.

Custer's arms enveloped Carmencita and it was impossible not to notice the affection he held for a young woman whose complexity I have only recently begun to credit. When he saw me looking at them, he dropped his arms. As if I care.

Danny and Dottie Dorino were holding on to Grace, who was convinced her body had gotten used to the water temperature, but who once again snapped, "Get me out!" the second the water reached her knees.

We are staying in three plywood buildings constructed on the site of Eugene O'Neill's dune shack, from the early days of the Provincetown Theater. Grace was so excited when she found out, she started collecting bits of brick and mortar locals say are the remnants of its foundation. Our provisions will last three days. For dinner this evening, we have bought fresh lobster and mussels. No propane out here. Just charcoal. Mr. Welsh and Leo have not yet decided who is to take charge of the fire.

Mr. Welsh is more comfortable with Leo than Leo is with him. They have not started talking business, but it is easy to see where the power lies. I have only to hear Leo say things like, "As you yourself pointed out, Mark," and I can imagine Lenore saying, "Ass-kisser!" The only time Mr. Welsh loses control, barely noticeably, is on the rare occasion Leo puts his arm around Maria. This almost never happens, but when it does, I see the corner of Mr. Welsh's mouth twitch.

Our wine supply will last four days if we do not continue to drink with as much enthusiasm as we have begun to this evening.

Dottie Dorino is bartending. She is saying how nice it is to get away from little Billy and Lizzie Dorino. Kids are great, don't get me wrong, she said. *Everybody* should have them. But after a dozen games of Candyland you're *dying* to know what adults are talking about.

Dottie tried to get Mr. Welsh and Leo to talk about their work. "It sounds *so interesting!*" she said. Then she smiled at Mr. Welsh, and looked toward her husband for approval.

"Honey, why don't you let me bartend?" is what he said. And Dottie looked hurt.

Leo, along with Mr. Welsh and Custer, ordered beers. Mrs. Dorino resumed her bartending, minus the commentary. Carmencita asked Dottie for a glass of white wine, but I intercepted it. Normally I do not drink, but for some reason I instinctively wanted to protect the baby Carmencita might decide to keep.

The wine went straight to my head. All barriers disappeared and the sunset, the surf, and the conversations at twilight poured right through me: I felt like an enormous vessel, CAPACITY—my middle name!—whatever it was, I was ready to hear, receive, confront, and feel it! I remembered the button a drinking buddy of John's once gave him: I DRINK TO MAKE OTHERS MORE INTERESTING. And I marveled at how even Grace's conversation did not annoy me.

"According to the book, that bird over there is a heron you don't see too often in this area." Grace put her bird book down and flipped through her plant guide. "As for these," she stood up with some difficulty in the unyielding sand, "these," she pointed to a waxy, cranberry-colored fruit, "are rosehips."

I jumped up to join Grace by the rosehips. The wine had taken over completely, making me fearless among the brambles. One part of me whispered, You'll feel the scratches tomorrow, but another did not stop me from pulling off a basketful of rosehips. Grace says you can eat them. But even if they had been poison, my newfound recklessness would have made me try just about anything. I dug my thumbnail through the rosehip's tough skin and split open what looked like a tiny pomegranate. Seeds all over the place.

"If enough of them are ripe, we'll make jam," Grace said. And that sounded reasonable. As I split rinds and ate rosehips at a furious rate, everything Grace was saying sounded reasonable.

I turned toward the ocean and took in the scene all at once. The wine had seized all appetites. With goodwill toward my travel companions and a surge of energy that made me want to experience everything first-hand, I ran down to the sea and cartwheeled in the surf. Hand-foot-hand-foot, I reminded myself. Anything seemed possible, even though I had not cartwheeled since before I had gotten sick. Hand-foot-hand-foot. The sea was sharp with cold. I started on firm sand, but the waves quickly pulled me toward the mouth of a bottomless, endlessly folding undertow. I was swallowed up and spewed out so quickly, the entire process took no longer than a scream.

The next thing I knew I had been thrown on my neck and could not move. My body was frozen and I could scarcely breathe. Sea gravel plugged every opening. An orange ball of fire revealed itself to me at rhythmic intervals, and a circle of faces, blurred by fright and a watery blanket, came sharply into focus as the sea retreated. For a moment my mother and father were among the people standing over me. Everybody was shouting. One voice broke through.

"DON'T MOVE HER!"

It was Custer yelling at Carmencita. I watched Carmencita's white bathing suit with black splotches split away from the rest, as if forming a new cell.

"GET AWAY! EVERYONE GET AWAY!"

The palest face refused to move. "Can you move, Meredith?" it asked.

When I tried to answer, the water covered me again, heaping more gravel in my mouth, my eyes, my nose.

My limbs were locked.

This is it, I thought. Paralyzed. Let me drown right here rather than spend my life in a wheelchair. After the panic, they say, drowning is very peaceful.

"Dig her out!" the pale one ordered. It was the face I knew least until my mind told me it was Leo. Leo was telling Custer and Mr. Welsh to dig under my body. Maria was crying hysterically as she removed the sand from my face, but she disciplined her shaking hands long enough to help me breathe. Every time the surf came up again, undoing her work and embedding me further, she screamed, "Hurry up!—She can't breathe!" and renewed her convulsive sobbing.

I do not know how much longer it was before I felt pressure

on my right palm. Carmencita had been rubbing it with a vengeance—slapping it, squeezing it, pulling at my fingers, blowing on them to warm them up, until finally, she saw my index finger trying to wave at her.

Carmencita shouted, "She moved her finger!"

Immediately afterwards, Leo shouted, "Okay, let's lift her!"

I have no memory of what happened after that. The next thing I knew Grace was wrapping me in a warm blanket and Mrs. Welsh was playing with my legs and arms.

"Frozen solid," Mrs. Welsh was saying to Custer. "She's fine. Just frozen solid."

"Is she gonna be okay?"

"She's gonna be just fine. Lots of scratches, but this young lady's got more life in her than all of us put together."

I was too exhausted to even acknowledge the comment. Except, of course, by the routine salutation from my tear ducts. Mrs. Welsh's voice was so tender I cried and cried as she rubbed my arms and legs. Immediately my emotions were interpreted as fear and trauma from the cartwheel incident. And there was plenty of that. But with our most concentrated tears, we are always crying for ourselves *and* others.

I felt sorry for Mrs. Welsh. How hard this vacation must be for her! All I could do was pray that her mother's visit would give her solace. With any remaining energy, I acknowledged the general kindness my accident had brought out in everyone. And I felt like a hypocrite after everything I had said about them. People say beautiful things when they either assume you are about to die, or, in this case, think you cannot hear.

And they *mean* them.

I do not like being the center of attention. And when I am, and when people display the kind of love and affection that makes them almost unrecognizable, I cannot stop crying.

I sniffled and thawed out for the rest of the evening. Everyone came in to talk to me, politely spacing their visits, and only the unfrozen part of me—my brain—received them properly. My brain said—consulting with my heart, that is—my brain said that if people were as kind and as gentle as they are capable of all the time, the world would drown in tears of awkward gratitude.

19.
If a Body Meets a Body

I am respectful of the surf today, and embarrassed to remember myself at the center of the ordeal a couple of days ago.

Since then our attention has turned from the sacred—a life in peril—to the mundane—fleas and sanitation. Mark Welsh did not tell us there is no plumbing out here. So, while everyone is trying to be polite, some of the dune shacks—his in particular—smell like the human version of low tide.

Nobody mentioned fleas, either. For some reason they have taken the greatest liking to Mr. Welsh. His ankles are spotted from last night's battle with the microscopic pests. "YOUCH—goddamn it! Louisa?—are they getting you or just me!" Carmencita, who shares a plywood partition with me, laughs when she hears him in the neighboring shack. "*Me encanta, este hombre, me encanta,*" she says. "He would be furious if he found out anybody were laughing at him," I say. Then we listen to another round of "YOUCH—goddamn it—Louisa!" and tend to our own, less severe bites.

By lunchtime things got a bit tense. The men were unshaven, thirsty, flea-bitten, and with the exception of Custer and Leo, they stank. The women were not much better. I do not mean to be catty, but in times like these you notice when a woman has a mustache. Carmencita left her bleach at home, and while this in no way diminishes her beauty, it has changed her face considerably.

Grace announced she had an appointment in Provincetown and started bossing everybody around. "Welsh—why don't you head into town with me and buy groceries, water, bug repellant, and candles for tonight? Leo!—how about digging an outhouse? Custer!—help him out. Meredith!—Carmen!—collect the trash and dig a hole for it. We'll help out when we get back."

Grace spared Louisa, and she did not touch the Dorinos, because it was clear that Dottie and Danny were not dressed to do anything but shop. Dottie was wearing an electric blue cotton sweater with stitches wide enough to let gales through. And her husband's Italian loafers had no place on the dunes.

Six hours later, an annoyed Mr. Welsh returned with supplies. The only shopping contribution Grace had made was the scrimshaw ring she was waving around proudly, and the Dorinos had checked into a hotel in Provincetown.

For all his experience digging ditches in Thailand, Mr. Welsh contributed very little to the final stages of the outhouse, but we finished all our chores, expertly—motivated, as we were, by a common disgust.

The physical labor left everyone exhausted. After an early dinner prepared by Louisa, Leo and Mark Welsh drifted off to discuss the state of the world. I could hear them trying to get along. A strong statement by one was followed by an equally loud HA-HA by the other. Custer called it "the distinct sound of male bonding." And Maria felt left out. I wanted to butt my head between Leo and Mr. Welsh and shout: That son-of-a-bitch Welsh probably got you fired, but I do not care enough about Leo to get involved. He bores me.

The rest of us went into the dune shack I share with Carmencita, Maria, and Grace. We started a game of Scrabble. Grace went to bed after her first word and Louisa was trying to read a new Balanchine biography by candlelight. Everyone's efforts were subverted; no one was experienced with candlelight. The dimmest bulb I had ever read under was forty watts, which, by comparison, was like reading in the Hall of Mirrors at Versailles. I know candlelight makes everyone look good—and Custer was looking pretty steamy—but it did nothing for our game. After twenty minutes, we all gave up and went in separate directions.

I headed for the dunes. The moon was full, casting a sharp white line from the horizon to the shore. On either side, the light was more diffuse and buffed from its exchange with the sea. As I watched, a voice from behind called out, "Green quartz."

I turned my head and saw Custer's tall, athletic silhouette.

"Isn't that what it looks like, Red? Or maybe talc, where the water gets shallow."

Custer's voice was soft and intense. And for some reason I was incredibly nervous. When he sat down beside me it was not the way an acquaintance sits next to an acquaintance. Nor was it like a buddy sitting next to a buddy. It was more the way a body meets a body coming through the rye, or, in this case, the sea grass.

Custer seemed preoccupied, but at the same time kinetically predisposed toward me. The next thing I knew he was introducing himself to my neck. He nudged me playfully with the top of his head, then traversed my nape with a series of slow kisses which warmed me up considerably.

I squirmed around a little until I felt comfortable in his arms. Then for the hell of it I attacked his mouth. "Youch!" he cried.

My embarrassment made me mortally silent. I tried to break the seal Custer's strong arms had me locked in, but he would not let me. I dug my head into his chest and announced that I would suffocate right there if he did not let me go. Custer called my name a few times, and finally succeeded in getting my attention.

"Red?"

"What?"

"Try again."

"No."

"Why?"

"You *know* why. I'm embarrassed."

I still had not come up for air. And my voice was so muffled, Custer had a hard time understanding me.

"I can't hear you," he said.

I lifted my head. His face was white from the moon's reflection, the same eerie look as someone watching a black-and-white television in the dark.

"You *know* why," I said.

"Try again," he repeated.

Had the face been more repulsive, had the lips been less inviting, I might never have tried again. But Custer looked so kind and patient, I gave him the most professional kiss I knew how—one which, I can only speak for myself, made all the electrons in my body orbit more frantically.

As for the magnetic bond between my chest and Custer's,

that was broken when he uncoiled my body and lay me flat in the sand. His movements seemed to gather strength and resolve—so much so that Custer had begun to hurt me. His hands were kneading my body with a pressure too hard to withstand and, when I cried out, Custer stopped for a moment—his face looked exceedingly troubled—and started up again. He dug his face into my body and continued even more furiously, making his way down to the zipper on my cheetah. Up and down he zipped and unzipped my bathing suit until, suddenly, I felt his mouth pressing against my skin and almost biting me. "Custer!" I shouted, "you're hurting me!"

As soon as I had uttered the words, Custer's body relaxed, and I felt warm tears against my chest. Even though Custer had roughed me up, something told me to stroke his hair and make a general display of my affection for him. He cried for a while, then—once, gently—kissed my side before zipping me up.

I felt sorry for Custer. Since the discovery of his father's suicide, anger and frustration mark his every move. Though he says I am his favorite human, I worry about becoming the focus of everything he is going through. He has pulled inside himself like a turtle, withdrawing to question his very existence. When he pokes outside to acknowledge me, he often snaps.

"Red?"

"What?"

"I'm sorry."

"It's okay."

"Red—"

"What?"

"I think I press against you very hard because I don't want you to leave me."

I sighed a very long sigh. Then I told Custer he really had to stop being such a morbido.

"Custer," I said, "I'm not *going* anywhere."

"When's your checkup?"

"January."

"You feelin' okay?"

"Fine."

"Are you sure?"

"Positive."

"You're *lookin'* fine." He reached over wearily to pinch a cheetah spot and snapped the fabric in the moonlight. On further inspection, Custer's body stiffened. I knew what he was thinking.

"What's the matter?" I asked.

"Nothing I should bother you with."

"It's *already* bothering me. What is it?"

"The bathing suit—"

"Same one as Carmencita's?"

Custer was silent. Then he said, "You guessed it."

I was discouraged. Especially since the interruption made me conscious of the fact that what we had been doing was the preamble to the way Carmencita got pregnant. Lust and prudence suddenly collided, then a layer of general yuk smothered my fragile excitement as I thought of Custer's problems.

When I sat up, Custer put his arms around me and asked if I was okay.

"Fine," I said. "*Great!*"

"Red?"

"What?" I wriggled out of Custer's arms, and established myself next to him, solid and independent as a telephone pole.

"Red, I'm sorry."

"Forget about it."

"I like you a lot—"

"I don't want to hear about it."

"I don't just like you. I'm *attracted* to you."

"*Really?*" I said sarcastically.

"Yes, *really*," he said, matching my tone. "But I've got to sort things out with Carmencita first." He paused to read my face. "In fact, I've got a whole lot of things to sort out. Know what I mean?"

"Sure do."

"What's that supposed to mean?"

"Just what I said. Sure do—I'm agreeing with you."

"You've got that sneering tone. If you were Carmencita, wouldn't you want me to respect your feelings before I got involved with someone else?"

"Sure would."

"That's enough!"

"*But who says we're going to be involved?*"

Custer snatched my shoulders and made me face him. "You know, Red, I'm beginning to understand why Jonathan roughed you up—"

"I roughed *him* up—"

"Well, I'm beginning to understand his frustration—"

"I don't have to listen to this—"

"No, you don't. But if it's me tellin' you, you might want to think about it!"

"What makes *you* so special?"

"Oh shut up! I've had it."

Custer jumped up and headed for the dune shack he shared with his parents. I watched his strong back recede, looking a little discouraged around the shoulders. As Custer got farther away, my instincts told me that my friendship as well as any amorous future with Custer were at stake.

I ran so fast, the sand squeaked like rubber.

"Custer?"

He did not turn around.

"Custer!"

"What?"

"I'm sorry."

"Forget it."

"No. I don't want to forget it. I want to apologize."

I went up to him, arms crossed against my chest, head bowed, and waited for him to hug me. He would not do it.

"Red, I don't have the strength for this sort of thing."

We were silent for a while, breathing air in like a sea tonic. Finally, I spoke with a voice filled with hurt. "When you talk to Carmencita, make sure you ask how she's doing."

Custer said he would, then turned to leave because he thought I was changing the subject.

When I called after him, he would not turn his back.

20.

Looking for Grace and A Conversation with Maria

I blew it last night, and I have been sulking all day—so much so that when Maria came into the shack to tell me that Grace was missing I did not believe her.

We had been with Grace last night. She had licked her chops during the Scrabble game, annoying us with the sound a dog makes when he is cleaning his teeth.

I had seen her this morning. She was eating granola with condensed milk and making that hay-munch noise that drives me crazy.

Grace had missed lunch, which is unusual; but Maria had not started worrying until now. It is 4:00 P.M. Louisa and Custer are taking a walk. Carmencita went fishing with Leo and Mr. Welsh. And Maria and I started off in the opposite direction, west, to look for Grace.

I know what probably happened. The nearest dune house is a half-mile away. Grace wandered by, chatted up the neighbors. Maybe they drove her into town. Grace is so unpredictable and so independent, Maria and I cannot foreclose any possibilities.

We scanned the beach, and did not see a single person walking in either direction. If Grace had ventured east, our fishermen would find her. And if she had really gone far in that same direction, Louisa and Custer would catch up with her, since they had started out even earlier.

From where we were, an expanse of sand, sea, sky, and compass grass was occasionally relieved by clumps of mysterious debris which revealed themselves on approach. Helmets in the sand became hermit crabs; translucent cockscombs with hot pink piping swiftly turned to man-o'-wars; licorice whips turned out to be a robust seaweed Maria and I had never seen before.

Concerned as I was about Grace, I was not really worried —nor was Maria. I was caught up in my own problems, wishing I could take back last night's developments. Maria snapped me out of myself long enough to make me look forward to our walk as a way of continuing a number of conversations we had never finished. She was surprised by Mr. Welsh's behavior. "I guess I expected a blow-up," she said.

"Are you disappointed?"

"Not really. Confused, maybe. I underestimated how controlled he is."

"Custer said he went to West Point."

"Maybe that's it."

"Lenore says millionaires can't afford to lose their tempers or fall in love. If they divorce, the wife takes half of what they're worth."

"He told me."

"What do you mean, he told you?"

"Mark met with his accountant, who told him that love and lust are well and good, but if you're worth a few million you should either cross your legs or stay married and have affairs."

"How's Leo?"

"Well, I hate to say this—"

"What?"

"Lenore's right."

"Ass-kisser?"

"I hate to admit it. But it's hard to respect somebody who's brown nosing the man who probably got him fired. It's kind of pathetic to see Leo going out of his way to please a man he doesn't even respect. All because he's looking for a job and thinks Mark might be helpful." Maria smiled. "Lenore's right about another thing—"

"What's that?"

"Last night Leo played me a tape of some songs he had written."

"And?"

"He's no musician."

"Bad?"

"Awful. Absolutely awful."

"So who's on first?"

"What do you mean?"

"You know, which one do you want now?"

Maria sighed one of those bottomless sighs and got a little teary. "You know that line—*A great hope fell. You heard no noise. The ruin was within.* Well, that's the way I feel about both of them." She started to cry, and looked so helpless I reached over to pat her on the back. "We'll find you someone else," I said.

"I'm sick of them all!" Maria shouted. She wiped her eyes with the back of her hand, and a few seconds later remarked, "For all her advice, do you know the *real* reason Lenore's not here?"

"Because she hates Mark Welsh, would have murdered him on the dunes and left him here to rot."

"No. Because John's visiting her and the kids."

"No way!"

"It's true." Maria stepped to the side to avoid a dead jellyfish, then resumed. "She said something the other day that floored me. She was talking about John. She said that she's got the jargon down: He's an alcoholic; she's a codependent. Monstro and Elizabeth are the children of alcoholics so they also have the disease. There's only one problem, she said—and this—" Maria turned toward me suddenly. "This is what I *love* about Lenore. She said, there's only one problem. I asked, 'what's that?' The problem, she said, is that John is and will always be the love of my life."

I smiled inside. It sounded just like Lenore.

"She went on and on about AA. They teach you to recognize that it's not your fault and they're incredibly supportive. But she wondered if, in some cases—in some minute cases—whether the love so outweighs the illness that, in the case of someone who is functional, and not a drunk you have to carry home. In other words, in the less obvious cases—the case of a man who is, on the whole, a good father, a good husband, but who—let's be honest, she said—is dependent. Who relies on one glass of wine at lunch and two glasses of wine at dinner. A man who, yes, medicates himself—*'I'm not denying it!'*—she said. In the case of such a man, what if I love him and still want him back?"

"So what did you say?"

"I told her she had articulated the most pressing question of this century, if not of all time."

I smiled. "Are there others?"

"Plenty."

"Like what?" I dipped down to pick up a stick of driftwood which, I was convinced, would help me concentrate on what Maria was about to say.

"Well. How about, 'Who is Grace, where is she, and why in God's name is she not listed along with fire and hurricanes as one of the great forces of nature?'"

We both laughed, in a moment of fondness for Grace, who singlehandedly caused more ulcers than anyone we had ever met. We agreed that Grace's acidic powers came from her unfiltered directness. "I can't wait to be eighty-six and say exactly what I want," I said.

Maria pointed to the nearest dune shack, which was still about a ten-minute walk.

"Do you think she's all right?" I asked.

"Definitely," Maria reassured me. "She's probably trying to call Mr. Sneff. But she could have saved herself the trouble. No phones out here."

We started climbing up the ridge of sand, behind which a dune shack—presumably owned by an artist, since it had Gauguin-type murals painted all over it—held a precarious vertical. On the way up, Maria asked about Custer. "He's awfully edgy lately," she commented. "I don't remember him having such a short fuse. I asked him a question yesterday, and he acted like a dog who had been kicked too many times."

"What did you ask him?"

"I don't even remember. Something about Grenada. He thought I was prying about his dad—"

"He's going through a lot," I interrupted.

"Because of Carmencita?"

"No."

"Because of you?"

"In part."

I blushed, which, to Maria, confirmed everything. "C'mon, tell me," she pressed. "Are you due for my big sister lecture on safe sex—"

"Maria! I really don't want to talk about it. He's kind of a mess right now."

"I'm sorry." Maria stopped probing. "Anything I can do?"

"Yes."

"What?"

"Don't ask him about his father."

"Deal," she said firmly. Then Maria muttered, "Poor kid. I just hope Louisa and Mark don't do permanent damage. Louisa's sweet, but a little out of touch—"

"MARIA! The woman is in pain! Even if nothing has happened between you and her husband. She sees the way he looks at you—"

"I know that!"

My shouting had rattled Maria. She collapsed into the sand, and I remained standing. "Sit down, Meredith," she commanded in a quiet, firm voice. I really wanted to stand. "Sit down," she repeated. I resisted, then finally plopped into the sand and awaited verbal excoriation.

"Look, don't think I don't feel for Louisa Welsh. I would feel for any woman who got herself into that position. Maybe she should have stayed in the South. Maybe she should have stayed married to her first husband. Maybe ballet was the wrong profession for her. Maybe she should work so she's not financially dependent on a man. Maybe she should say fuck you to Mark Welsh if he's such a louse. The point is that it's none of my business. And—if anything—I think I have acted somewhat admirably under the circumstances—"

"I didn't mean to suggest you hadn't—"

"Thank you. But I don't need your approval or disapproval. That home is *wrecked*, Meredith. And it has nothing to do with me. If there's anyone I really feel sorry for it's Custer. He needs a father every bit as much as Monstro and Elizabeth. I even understand Lenore's confusion—John drinks, but he's a great father. The one thing I despise about Mark Welsh is his selfishness. He wants all the attention in his marriage and, up until now, that's where Louisa's been putting most of her energy—"

"She loves Custer—"

"*Of course she loves Custer!* And she loves Mark Welsh. That's not the point! The point is she'd be a lot better off if she cared about herself a little more—and so would they, for that matter."

"Maria?"

"What?"

"I didn't mean to suggest you were a home wrecker or anything. And if I gave you that impression I'm very sorry. As for Custer, I'm very worried about him."

"Well, I'm not going to drag it out of you. If you want to talk about it, you know where to find me." Maria stood up. "C'mon, let's get Grace." She started walking toward the shack.

"Maria?"

My sister turned around.

"I *do* want to talk to you. Not yet. But I want to talk to you."

Maria pulled me out of the sand, patted me on the back, smiled, and said, "Never keep a force of nature waiting!"

21.

Grandmother Is Gone

Still no sign of Grace.

Oswaldo the artist said she had stopped by his shack, looking for a phone, so there was nothing to worry about.

That was six hours ago.

Afterwards, we returned to our settlement and dispatched new search teams. I have never witnessed a more committed team. Leo, Custer, and Louisa divided up the shoreline. Maria, Carmencita, and I took the dunes. And Mr. Welsh drove the jeep into Provincetown to see if the Dorinos had heard from her. We raced against the darkness, taking every probable or improbable turn. When the sun finally dropped beneath the horizon, the blink of orange took with it our only hope for finding Grace before morning.

Mr. Welsh returned from Provincetown with no news of Grace. The Dorinos had checked out of their hotel yesterday and, when Mr. Welsh called them in Mainsfield, they said they had not seen Grace.

"Did you call Mr. Sneff?" I asked.

He had not.

We ate our last dinner on the dunes and decided to pack our things. We would file a report with the Provincetown coast guard and police, and resume a final search tomorrow morning before checking into a hotel in Provincetown.

To his credit, Mr. Welsh never suggested we split up. He could easily have returned to Mainsfield to work on his best-seller. Leo could have begged out as well. And while ultimately both of them wanted to be with Maria—though it was impossible to tell by the way they behaved on this trip!—I think the higher sentiment was based on a concern for Grace.

"Do you think she's okay?" I asked Louisa, before going to bed.

"I'm sure she is," Louisa replied.

Custer was worried, and I did not want to hear it. Too much death on the brain distorts what we all believed was a realistic optimism.

"Do you think she's okay?" I asked Carmencita before we went to bed.

"*Seguramente!*" she said. And when she took her clothes off, I noticed with fright how big her breasts had grown, and how her stomach was distended.

I lay awake most of the night, listening to the waves pound the shore, and worrying about Carmencita and Grace. They were the most infuriating women I had ever met. I thought about Carmencita's parents. I thought about my parents. We had to find Grace before my father came home. You cannot have a man's mother disappear on him while he is in Europe.

I figured out what I admire about Carmencita and Grace. They are alive. They take risks. Grace's are more calculated, but she is a lot older. I like the way they churn things up, even if they unsettle entire populations in their wake.

After hours of imploring the plywood ceiling for answers, I closed my eyes and surrendered to an exhausted peace—one that allowed me to catch a few hours' sleep.

Tomorrow, we will find Grace.

22.
Grace

I got up early and tried not to wake Maria and Carmencita. The air was blue-grey, before the sun had poked through, and unseasonably chilly.

I had not wanted to wake up. In my dream a dog was being suffocated by two people who never turned their backs. I stood by helplessly, opening my mouth to scream, with no screams coming out. Then I began to have trouble breathing. What felt like a fist pressed against the center of my chest prevented me from getting enough air.

So when the sea wind ballooned inside by chest, I was feeling pretty optimistic—about the restorative powers of the ocean and the regenerative powers of my grandmother. I knew we would find her; it was just a matter of time. In fact, I would not have been surprised to see her walking from the direction of Oswaldo's shack, in time to meet us for breakfast.

I walked down to the shoreline, and found the Atlantic less frightening than usual. The waves slapped the sand with the same force they always had, but somehow, the ocean seemed friendlier—maybe because the water was warmer than usual, and because the sea foam had the consistency of meringue.

I waded in up to my ankles, then my calves. I would not go

any further; the undertow was mighty, throwing out shells, sand, and, occasionally, foreign objects that made me jump with fright.

I do not know how long I stood in the surf before Carmencita came to join me. She was smiling in a way that made me think she had decided to have the baby. As I thought about that, the fist pressed against my chest again. What seventeen-year-old could make that decision by herself? I wondered how her parents would advise her. If a baby is in the works, Catholics generally want to keep them around. Carmencita would have to tell someone eventually. Someone other than me. The burden of a confidence I had never solicited was overwhelming. And as I watched Carmencita scoop up sea water in her hands to wet her face, I tried to picture that same beautiful face —not as a teenager, but as a mother. I could see it. But how it would change her life!

My thoughts were interrupted by Carmencita's romp in the surf. "It's warm today, Meredith—just when we have to leave!" she cried. And no sooner had Carmencita made the observation than the sun's rays began heating up the air and siphoning off the greyness.

"Are you packed?" I asked.

"*Absolutamente!*"

"That means yes?"

Carmencita smiled. "You know it does. Your Spanish has gotten a lot better thanks to me." She let out a little scream as a branch of driftwood hit her ankle. "Scared me!" she cried.

"There's all sorts of stuff floating around. What's everybody else up to?"

"They're awake. Packing. Mrs. Welsh is making pancakes. *Mi amor* Marco is eating them—"

"Just what he needs. Are you over him?"

"Oh, Meredith, don't you ever *dream* about anything! You're always so practical."

"I had a dream last night—about a dog that was being suffocated—"

"*No me interesa*—I don't want to hear it!"

I jumped. Something had slapped me in the legs. "I'm getting out!" I shouted.

I watched Carmencita enjoy herself. I had stopped wearing my cheetah bathing suit after the incident with Custer. Carmencita had not. "I'll be out in a minute, Meredith," she called. I sat down and played with a long shell shaped like an old razor blade. I carved out my initials. And just as I was writing Custer's name in the sand, Carmencita let out a blood-chilling scream.

I jumped up and shouted, "What's the matter?"

Scream after scream came from Carmencita's mouth. She would not stop.

I ran over to collect her, but could barely move her because she was stiff with horror. I immediately thought she was having a miscarriage and tried to carry her out of the surf. I could not lift her, and was constantly kicking off a substantial branch of driftwood that was hooking itself around my left leg.

On hearing Carmencita's screams, Custer and the others ran down to the shore. "What's the matter?" Custer yelled.

I told him I did not know. When he ran in to help me, I told him to be careful. And when he was too rough, I shouted all sorts of things to get him to be more gentle. I do not think the words "she's pregnant" slipped from my mouth, but I cannot promise anything.

All of a sudden Custer started shouting, too. For a moment his face froze in the shout position.

"*What?*" I yelled, "WHAT IS IT?"

I gave a final kick to what had been alternately flapping and clinging to my leg. When Carmencita was safely out of the water, I looked down to inspect the debris. At first I could not make it out. Then I did not want to. The source of Custer and Carmencita's hysteria suddenly became apparent to me as I watched a human hand retreat into the undertow.

In disbelief I watched the lip of the undertow disgorge the hand—then the arm it was connected to—then my grandmother's entire body was spewed onto the beach. She was virtually naked, stripped and scraped by the ocean. She was bloated, stiff as ivory, bloodless and unrecognizable.

"Good Lord, Gracie!" Mr. Welsh cried.

Nobody else spoke.

Custer disappeared for a moment and returned with Grace's bathrobe, which he gently threw over her surf-mauled body.

23.

Where the Air Is

I do not know how long I stared at Grace's body. All I remember is that, despite the robe Custer had covered her with, I continued to see the more graphic sight of Grace's nakedness. I could not stop looking at her fingers, which the robe had not quite covered. The whalebone ring seemed ghoulish. And her right hand, which I pictured choosing Scrabble letters, looked more like a chicken's foot. I started feeling what I thought had been a branch slapping against my leg and my muscles retained the memory of kicking it away. Suddenly my leg began kicking once more!—in a desperate effort to rid my brain and body of the memory.

No matter how many times I kick or try to forget, my body will not let me. Even when I dream, the memory seems locked inside the muscles that have committed the gruesome act. Last night I tried to calm down, vowing that I would not reconstruct the events, but, as soon as I closed my eyes, my grandmother's face appeared to me.

I wondered if I might have saved her. The hand around my ankle—had it been the clasp of a dead woman, or that of my grandmother seeking help? The idea that I might have saved her, coupled with the memory of her grasp, set off a wave of nausea. I ran out of the room I shared with Maria (we ended up staying two nights in Provincetown), hoping the sea air would settle my mind and stomach. But soon I started shrieking more desperately than either Custer or Carmencita.

I screamed at the top of my lungs until I could no longer breathe. And when I had swallowed new air I started up again. I screamed until the world was a single scream, with no other sound capable of penetrating the horror. I screamed until finally Maria ran out after me and struck me in the face to get me to stop. I was not even aware that Louisa had come out too. She was squeezing me as hard as she could to get me to calm down. I shoved Louisa away and started running toward the pier. I ran toward the emptiness, the openness—where the air was.

24.
Otis Redding and the Ice Pick

The first thing we did when we got back was to try to reach my father. We did not succeed because my parents are on their way home—this final week was not planned and therefore not on the itinerary they left us.

There is a hole in our house today. I shuffle around, confronted by reminders of my grandmother. Her extra pair of reading glasses, the passages she has notched in her travel books, the sound track of *Camelot* still on the turntable—and her Princess hair dryer, plugged into the wall upstairs, the bonnet waiting for Grace.

For one brief and perfect moment, everything was back to normal. Maria played an Otis Redding recording Mr. Welsh had bought her and Custer suddenly popped up and started dancing. It was not exactly a dance. It was a physical interpretation of the anguish Otis was singing about—

Pain in my heart!
(and Custer identified the actual spot)
Is treatin' me cold!
(Custer shivered and shimmied to his knees)

A more subdued supplication came with *Where can my baby be? No one knows.* This went on for the duration of the song until the *Pain in his heart* just wouldn't let him be! He would wake restless—

Lord! I can't even sleep!

Maria and I were captivated by the agile movements of Custer's tight body. He moved to the beat with grace and precision, and when the part came about how in other days he began to get rough, Custer let out a Ho! then a Yeeeaah! —before he cried—

Said I want you to
love me, love me, love me, baby—
'til I get enough!

As the song wound down, Custer made it clear that his heart and Otis Redding's were one. And where they merged, Maria and I found undeniable charm, feeling, and life knowledge. Which is why I think they call all this the blues.

Soon after, Custer and I went to visit Carmencita. Her flirt muscles are not working, but other than that, she seems okay. I was the one who finally told Custer he should call Carmencita. When I left, I heard her crying, with a sad Custer saying very little. Then Carmencita told Custer he had better leave before her parents came home from work.

Mr. Sneff came over today to pay his respects and ask about the funeral. I overheard him whisper specifics to a disconsolate Lenore. She told Mr. Sneff that we cannot bury Grace until my parents come home. He offered to call the local dry ice company and inquire about preservation. Most funeral homes do not handle dry ice and Mr. Sneff says we might have to keep Grace somewhere else, with a professional coming in to maintain her. He suggested our basement, the coolest part of the house. But Grace would hate that.

I thought Mr. Sneff had lost his mind, but since I have learned they eat mud in Mississippi, nothing surprises me. When Mr. Sneff offered to take care of Grace's funeral arrangements, I shouted, "NO!" from where I was eavesdropping on the porch and ran into the kitchen. I smiled grandly, welcoming Mr. Sneff, turned to Lenore and said, speaking for both of us—"Thank you very much. Grace was very fond of you. It's *very* kind of you to offer. But we'll take care of it."

Sneff hung around like he had a right to be there. I saw Custer out back and waved him toward our back door.

"Anything else, Mr. Sneff?" I asked.

"Actually, yes," he said. Then he lit up a cigar.

I was about to quote chapter and verse about smoking in our house when Mr. Sneff turned to Lenore and said, "Delicacy has prevented me from bringing up a business matter regarding Grace. You see, we met in Provincetown before she so tragically met her fate and—" He pulled a letter out of his pocket. "Well. We got engaged."

Mr. Sneff held the letter in front of us. I recognized Grace's handwriting. Custer came in and yanked it from his hands.

Finally, Lenore piped up. "What is it?"

"A letter from Grace accepting his offer of marriage."

"Bought her the finest scrimshaw ring money can buy. The next day, God rest her sweet soul, she . . ."

"was murdered," Custer interrupted.

"Murdered!" I exclaimed.

"Congratulations, Mr. Sneff," Custer said slowly. "What you've just told us makes you a murder suspect."

Sometimes I do not know where words come from. In this case, from the very bottom of Custer's vessel, where words run clear and uncontaminated.

"Murder!" Mr. Sneff balked.

"That's right. I'd keep *real* quiet about that letter if I were you. 'Rich Fiancée Drowns On Honeymoon.' Sounds awfully suspicious, don't you think?"

"We had legitimate real estate investments. Grace would want me to see them through . . ."

"Still," Custer continued, ignoring Mr. Sneff, "you might get off because an accomplished murderer probably would have waited until *after* the marriage . . ."

Mr. Sneff looked alarmed. And I had never witnessed so elegant an example of Custer's Southern *sangfroid*.

"Now, if she changed her *will* on account of you—well, in *that* case, you might wanna leave town!"

"I've been called a lot of things," Mr. Sneff said, "but I'm no murderer!" He excused himself, abruptly, leaving the stink of his cigar in his wake.

Custer turned to Lenore and me said, "Annie and Buster are on the porch." Lenore got hysterical. She was convinced that Mr. Sneff had hung around the dunes after the ceremony and drowned Grace for her money.

"Do you think he did it?" I asked Custer.

"No way," he said.

"Then why was he sneaking around Provincetown with her?" Lenore asked.

"'Cause he and Gracie knew you'd launch a thermo-nuclear

war if they had shopped for rings and announced their engagement in Mainsfield." He tucked his shirt in and added, "I just wanted to clip his wings in case he was thinking of cashing in on Grace."

One hour later, Mr. Sneff returned and had the audacity to introduce himself to Custer's grandmother. He was carrying more of Grace's favorite mineral water, obviously for Annie Fourchette, since Grace's thirst has stopped forever. Lenore disappeared into our kitchen, emerging with an ice pick.

"Get off this property, you bloodsucker!" Lenore shouted.

Buster started barking.

"Lenore! No hard feelings!"

"Get off this property before your eyeball ends up on the end of this ice pick!"

Buster's barking was frantic, especially when Lenore held the ice pick high above her head and started a downward stab. Mr. Sneff caught her arm. He and Annie yelled for her to stop. Then Sneff grabbed Buster, and Annie started pummeling him with her fists. I was trying to wrest the squirming cocker spaniel from Mr. Sneff, who had gained control of the ice pick —but when people are in a rage the voltage in their brains makes every part of their body stronger. Lenore grabbed the clay pot in which her begonia was lovingly planted. Poor Buster was locked in our grocer's iron-clad grasp and it looked like Sneff was about to attack the dog with the thinnest, sharpest implement I have ever seen. THWACK! Lenore hit the side of my head by mistake. THWACK! She hit Sneff with greater force. He fell to the floor, stabbing poor Buster as he went.

My head was killing me, but nothing can compare to the pain Annie experienced when she saw Buster's blood trickle from the wound, matting the gentle curls on his fur. Her entire body started shaking. "I think he's okay!" I shouted. I ran next door to get Dr. Pederson, who specializes in humans. When I returned, Lenore was calling Sneff a *fucking asshole!* and was about to finish him off with the ice pick.

Dr. Pederson was horrified. "What the hell's going on around here?" He turned to Lenore and me. "Where are your parents?"

"On vacation," I explained.

He seemed furious at the state of our household and shouted, "Stop this nonsense!"

When he walked over to Mr. Sneff, Annie yelled, "Forget about him, Buster's been stabbed!"

"The dog'll be fine," Dr. Pederson said. "It's not fatal." He tapped around and checked Mr. Sneff's eyes. "Out cold," he said. "Who did it?"

"Me," Lenore said.

"With what?"

"This," I said. I picked a clay shard off the floor.

"Lenore, I know our children play together, and that my wife thinks a great deal of you, but I must tell you that I consider this behavior a bit unbalanced for a woman your age."

"Mr. Sneff's a dirty louse," I said in defense of Lenore. "He tried to kill Buster and he might have murdered our grandmother!"

After that, I think Dr. Pederson obeyed the Hippocratic Oath with a little less enthusiasm. While he ministered to the *vieux gigolo*, we took Buster to the vet.

25.

The Cheek Kiss

Custer called to get my side of the story and, after we had examined recent developments from every conceivable angle, the conversation drifted to other matters. His parents are in New York City tonight, so we were able to talk longer than usual. He asked how I was doing. I thought about it for a moment, then told him the truth.

"Lonely," I said.

"What's that?"

"I said I'm lonely."

"Oh."

"Did you say something?"

"I said, 'Oh.'"

We were silent for a few seconds, then Custer resumed. "I'm lonely, too."

After another brief pause, Custer invited me over for something he called a "hug date."

"What's that?" I asked.

"A hug date is particularly suited for lonely people. There is no obligation whatsoever on a hug date—other than to be moderately affectionate toward someone you care about."

As I listened, my cheek jammed against the touch-tone

squares in the receiver of our phone, sending an electronic chime from my house to Custer's.

"What's that?"

"A cheek kiss," I said, making it up. "A cheek kiss occurs when the cheek punches the touch-tones." I tried to talk as scientifically as Custer, and with the same mock detachment in my voice, I asked, "Now about this hug date—"

"Yes. Well, hug dates, as you've just demonstrated, usually begin with cheek kisses, and build their way up to a maximum commitment of two pairs of arms—one male, one female—connected in some way, shape, or form."

"I see."

"One of the key points, of course, is that the minimum age for a hug date is eighteen years old and the maximum is nineteen—"

"So we're the only ones on the Alphabet Streets eligible?"

"Exactly."

"And what guarantee does the female component of the hug date have that the male component will not alter this agreement in any way—" At this point, my cheek inadvertently punched the phone and Custer thanked me for the cheek kiss.

"Word of honor," Custer answered.

"And until what time tonight does this offer stand?"

"Midnight."

"The doors to the castle close at midnight?"

"That's correct."

"Will the various dogs be in attendance?"

"No."

"Is Annie up?"

"Fast asleep."

"May I consider this offer in the bosom of my deeply disturbed family?"

Custer laughed, then wondered what I meant. "You mean, *ask* them about it?"

"No. I mean just think for myself."

"Absolutely."

I decided not to go. I gave Custer's offer a great deal of thought. So much so that, for a solid hour, the refrigerator and I seemed the only two beings left on earth. I trusted Custer, but something held me back.

Maria and I have two shows to do for Custer's stepfather before my sister goes back to New York. *The Business Hour* is very successful and Maxwell Firestone has recently guaranteed Mr. Welsh a one-year contract for a new show called *Eurotalk 92*. When Mr. Firestone flew into Mainsfield on his own jet to announce the deal, our town went berserk. The local press suddenly found itself elbowing its way through a more aggressive pack of national reporters—one of whom turned out to be Leo, already free-lancing for a cable magazine! All of this went to Mr. Welsh's head. I had never seen him happier, and I have never seen anyone forget someone he said he loved more quickly.

Maria might as well not exist for Leo or Mark Welsh. But every time she thinks she is going crazy, I bring out the shoebox to remind her it is *his* problem, not hers. The shoebox—a *very* large one originally for boots—contains approximately one hundred letters, photographs, articles, and wine corks from Mr. Welsh's days as the greatest lover of all time. If his phone calls had been transcribed, I estimate we would need fifteen shoeboxes more, in which case we would have to move into a larger house.

These days Mr. Welsh pretends he does not know her. And my guess is that Louisa finally confronted Mr. Welsh.

"He's a coward," Lenore said when Maria confided in her. "Don't blame yourself. Look at John F. Kennedy," she added, out of the blue. "We know what the 'F' stands for!"

Lenore came into the kitchen, and sat down to talk to me.

"Dr. Pederson's right," she said. "I'm losing it." She stood up suddenly, and when she went to the refrigerator to get some pepperoni, I knew it was going to be a fairly long conversation. I was about to ask Lenore how she could eat that stuff at eleven o'clock at night, but instead I asked, "What are you going to do?"

"Get help if John wants to."

"And if he doesn't?"

"*I* will. I can't go around smashing every idiot who comes in my path!"

I smiled. "Why not?"

"BECAUSE THERE ARE TOO MANY OF THEM!"

We both burst out laughing and Maria came into the kitchen.

"What's so funny?" she asked. Maria, I could tell, *wanted* to hear something funny.

"Enter headcase number two!" Lenore said.

"Three," I said. "You forgot me."

"I can't wait to go back to New York—" Maria began with a sigh.

"Oh, *yes*," Lenore urged her on with false sympathy, "people are *so much* saner there!"

"*Much* more relaxed," I added.

"Very funny, you guys." Maria's combustion machine started up and in the midst of all this riotousness the phone rang. My sisters were laughing so hard they did not hear the first few rings. I answered the call and motioned Lenore and Maria to be quiet. Then I heard my father say, "Hi, honey!—Is that you, Maria?" "No, it's Meredith," I said. "Isn't it awfully early where you are?" My father said they were making the most of their last two days. He was calling to give us their flight information. He asked how things were going. "Fine," I said. "Let me put Lenore on."

Lenore was still wiping tears of laughter from her eyes. In the split second before she took the phone, we all looked at each other and, without speaking, determined that we should not tell them about Grace until they got home. Why ruin their vacation?

At a quarter to twelve, I went to bed, content that we had come to the same conclusion about *not* telling my parents. I was equally pleased with my resolve about Custer's offer and, for a few minutes, I was confident I had made the right decision. I sat in the dark, staring out the window opposite my bed. I had no drapes in my room, so the streetlamp cast a perfect rectangle on the wall above my bed. When I was a little girl, I played with shadow puppets on the makeshift screen. Tonight I was more curious about my silhouette, but every time I turned my head to catch it, of course it disappeared.

I skated to the window in my socks. It was so quiet on Highland I could hear the buzz from the streetlamp. I leaned out the window to see if the lights in Custer's house were out and, just as his room caught my eye, the yellow square extinguished itself. Only the lamp in the Pederson's kitchen was on, and, a few minutes later, that snuffed out also. The streetlight was too remote a suggestion of a human presence, and suddenly I felt alone in the darkness—so much so that I began to panic. I lay down and tried to stop my heart from beating so fast, but the feeling would not go away. I was too old to be afraid of the dark and too young to feel so desolate. I felt like a child masquerading as an eighteen-year-old, too proud to ask for help.

I had been an adult for as long as I could remember.

Even when I was sick, I found myself reassuring my parents and everyone concerned so they would not worry about me. Custer was the only one who cut through the leukemia and, rather than seeing me as a sick person about to die, stayed with me and called me his favorite human. Then he got frightened too.

When I am honest with myself I admit that sometimes I miss Custer so badly I think the loneliness will never go away. It pressures my eyes, makes me swallow hard, constricts my chest, and hollows out my stomach. Nowadays, Custer is either very kind and tender, or he snaps. It is as if a switch goes off and he cannot control himself. All this is complicated by the fact that a whole new set of feelings takes over when I think about Custer as a young man. Something shimmery happens. Like thousands of butterflies teasing, tickling, and fluttering their way into every corner of my weightless body. Then the center of my yearning migrates south of my brain and listens to some velvet heat that makes me want to smash against Custer.

This second feeling made me change my mind about tonight. I had missed Custer's deadline and I did not care. Something wild and powerful marched me out of my room and made me scamper lightly down the stairs like a cat burglar. I held my breath—as if that made a difference!—until I had successfully closed the screen door nearest our pond. Then the night met me with its own swirl of activity—frogs, birds, crickets—and silent splashers of the night! The breeze made paper wind chimes of the leaves, and, higher up, the wind seemed to whisk clouds past our first autumn moon. The air was cool, and everything alive ushered me toward the Welsh castle. Custer had kept the back door open, just in case, and when Rufus-Coco greeted me, even he seemed to know he should keep his woofer shut, just this once!

I winced at every creak on the stairs, and held my breath again. (Why do humans assume the world will be silent just because they are holding their breath?!) I did not knock on Custer's door. I walked in, quietly, and watched him sleep. He lay on his stomach, with his head turned toward the window. Every muscle in his bare back and arms suggested strength, yet in repose Custer looked vulnerable. Maria had a postcard of a man with the same torso; Caravaggio painted it. I straddled Custer's body on all fours and kissed his moonlit shoulders. He jumped—"Ha!"—not a laugh, but a cry of fright, then he turned slowly toward me. "That you, Red?" he whispered, half asleep. He reached for me as I lowered myself into his arms and kissed my cheek in welcome.

I was entirely convinced that I had found the warmest spot on earth. The covers were chastely still between us, so I lied to Custer. I told him I was cold.

At first he did not respond. Then he whispered, "Turn away a second, Red. I'll put my pajamas on so you can come under the covers."

I turned away, heard him open a drawer, and the next thing I knew he had hopped back into bed. "Okay," he said quietly.

"I can't go to bed with my clothes on," I said.

"She *can't* go to bed with her clothes on," Custer appealed to some ghost in the room.

"Do hug dates require me to go to sleep fully clothed?"

"I'm afraid they do."

"No exceptions?"

"Rarely."

"And in the *rare* event of exceptions, how do they work?"

Custer was waking up. "In *very* rare cases—when one of the parties is unhappy with the original agreement—the terms can be renegotiated."

"I would like that. I would also request that one more article of clothing be discussed—"

"What's that?"

"Raincoats."

"Pardon?"

"Raincoats. You know, those things men put on when it looks like it's going to rain—"

"I have one in the closet if you really want—"

"Hold on," I interrupted. Custer was not getting it, even though—according to Carmencita—he had originally coined the term. I really did not want to explain, so I foraged through his medicine cabinet and came out with a Trojan. I slipped it under Custer's pillow, and he reached under to feel what I was talking about.

"You really mean business," he said. He was quiet for a moment, then sat up, "You sure this is what you want?"

"Yes," I said.

"Red?"

"What?"

"Are you *positive?*"

I reached over and cupped Custer's mouth with my hand. *Stop asking* is what that meant. And because Custer is not stupid, he started kissing the palm I had offered him. Then he reached over playfully to feel what I was wearing. He must have seen the moonlight on my buttons because he seemed to know exactly where they were. He undid the first one and kissed the side of my neck. Then after a hungry excursion along my throat, his mouth made its way up to my face. He placed both hands on either side of my head, and swept my hair back. "I like you with your hair back, Red. You have a beautiful face."

I did not know where to look. Fortunately Custer had his own agenda. The next thing I knew he was kissing my mouth, my eyes, my forehead, and coaxing all sorts of mystery spots until the core to my reactor was on the verge of a meltdown.

There was only one bad moment when Custer's adeptness with zippers, hooks, and the usual entanglements made me jealous of all the zippers and hooks that had already come his way.

As for his pajamas—a formality at this point—circumstances obliged me to make short shrift of them. In the presence of his skin, which is the softest yet firmest human surface I have ever felt, I found myself addicted. I know that the first time you are intimate with someone a host of discomforts are supposed to ensue, but they did not. I felt warm, then warmer—and Custer's heat broke evenly like oil on a rind. His mouth, after pleasurable side trips to various parts of my body, would return to my face to ask how I was doing.

Just *fine*, thank you.

And because these are very personal things that really do not interest people, and because all this has been described at great length over the centuries *far* better than my limited experience can allow, I will only say that there is nothing more worthwhile on this planet than two people who care about each other expressing it in so purposeful and satisfying a manner.

Anyone who says otherwise is a liar.

Afterwards Custer held me very tight and I was thinking about what Maria had said about breaking through to someone's soul.

My sisters had warned me that men say all sorts of things after making love, and Custer was no exception. Nothing could have prepared me for the love assault coming out of Custer's mouth. "I love you, Red." Then later, "I'll go *crazy* if you tell me we can't do this again!" Followed by "Maybe we'll end up married." Above all he insisted that he had never, *ever*, been so physically compatible with *anyone*.

I did not want to know how many.

I listened to Custer talk in hushed, raptured tones about my eyes, my hands, my hair, my breasts, my skin.

You forgot my ankles, I said. I was very proud of my ankles.

Your ankles, your calves—and suddenly he began to invent code names for the more private parts of my body. Thighs became drumsticks, buttocks—"bunny slopes." I will not say what broccoli stood for. Then back to my smell, my voice, my nose, my eyelashes.

I thought I would never escape that love pit.

Every time I told Custer I had to go, I got a one-more-for-the-road argument. I cannot say that I minded—if anything I was amazed by how easily we were able to forget our troubles—but I do know that, with the various postponements, I could have gotten as far as Reno for sure.

After two repeat performances, I turned on my side, nestled under Custer's arm, whispered, "Give me a break!" and fell asleep against his quilted chest.

26.
The Tears of the World

Nature never finished Carmencita's baby. Not long after Custer and I saw her, Carmencita complained of fierce abdominal cramps. Mr. and Mrs. Alfonso brought her to the hospital, expecting that she would have her appendix removed, and learned that she was pregnant. At first they were furious. Then I think they were glad to know Carmencita was okay.

I hate to say this, but in a way maybe what happened is best for Carmencita and Custer, as well as for her parents. I have to believe that Grace's death had something to do with it. But there is a lot I do not know.

I do know that Carmencita's loss sometimes refrigerates my desire for Custer. And in the midst of all this, Jonathan came by to ask me how I was doing.

"Not so great," I said. "Grace's funeral will probably be on the day school starts."

"Do you want me there, or shall I take notes for you in school?"

"I want you to stop being nice to me. I'm not nice to you, so why should you be nice to me?"

"I don't know. I've been asking myself that while you were away. I should be angry with you. Especially since Custer was with you in Provincetown—"

"What's that got to do with it?"

"Come on, Meredith. I'm not stupid. He's the one you want and I'm *still* willing to be your friend."

"That's sick."

"Maybe. But Custer isn't exactly the picture of health lately."

I wanted to kick Jonathan again, but I restrained myself. The impulse was not to defend Custer, who, Jonathan was right, had grown restless and troubled, but to defend myself for getting involved with Custer under such complex circumstances.

"Who's your homeroom teacher?" I asked, trying to avoid World War III.

"I couldn't believe Custer yelled at *you* about Carmencita's—"

"Do you have Mr. Nichols for English again?"

"pregnancy—"

I pulled back a bit. "Jonathan," I began, speaking in the most controlled voice possible, "I'm sorry you heard all that stuff. Custer was upset no one had told him about Carmencita. But you know what? Even if you do know everything and even if you are *right* about everything, that's still not going to change one basic fact—"

"I know that—"

"And that fact is—"

"I know what it is!"

"The fact *is* that no amount of knowledge or persuasion—"

"Don't be cruel."

"*No amount of knowledge or persuasion* is going to make me attracted—"

"STOP!"

"*—attracted to you!*"

If the first leaf of autumn had fallen after this exchange, I would have heard it. The silence bore hardship, as well as the hollowness of victory. I did not want to be right about Jonathan any more than he wanted to be right about me. Deep down, we resemble one another.

We are sick of moral victories.

We want to be loved.

Jonathan was punctured by my comment. And after he left I felt very sad. I do not take love for granted, but I really do believe that Jonathan's affection is qualified in ways that make it impossible for us to be friends. The irony is that now, more than ever, I need a friend. How can Custer be my best friend now that we have been intimate?

I called Custer from the kitchen, and he said he would ring me back. Since I am particularly sensitive to anything Custer does right now, I immediately interpreted this as evidence of a rift. He used to drop everything to speak with me, but this time he claimed Rufus-Coco was fighting with Buster, and he had to de-jaw them.

I waited an hour for Custer's call. A reasonable amount of time to unclamp two dogs, I thought. Then I went for a walk on the aqueduct.

The dirt road is parched and curry-colored under foot. Mainsfield has not had rain in weeks, but when I look up, clouds gather with mottled speed, promising water. All I can think about is how sad and disappointed I am with everything and everybody. I am sure a lot of this has to do with being especially vulnerable to Custer. I expected him to be more communicative after what happened the other night.

Eight days have passed since Grace drowned and already I

miss her fiercely. I could not have expected this. And I am worried that my parents will think we behaved irresponsibly when they find out. But Grace is the type of person who was destined to die in the saddle. My father must know that.

As for Custer, we have always had a fiery friendship, one that repaired itself like an immune system in the body. If one of us was wounded, zillions of white blood cells would rush to the site correcting the problem.

Nowadays, neither of us is healing properly. When I do not hear from him, I no longer assume everything is okay. I am even beginning to question Custer's attraction to me. I can still feel the slow and tender progress his mouth and hands made on my body. I want that to happen again. But then I remind myself of what happened to Carmencita.

The air today is hot, humid, and thick as soup. On days like these, Custer and I used to insist that Grace stay in the air-conditioning. Now Vidalia's Funeral Home has her fixed up so that she will not feel a thing.

In my dream last night, Grace was asking me about Custer. If I piece it together properly, I can hear her saying, "Oh, for Christ's sake, Meredith—do *something* if Custer gave you a signal! Stop *thinking* so much!"

But Custer says that thinking is part of what moralists do. So, while my grandmother's advice is perfectly sound, I secretly and fanatically hope that all this thinking has, at the very least, made me a good moralist.

Whatever happens, I tell myself I have been through a lot worse. Or maybe I have not. I do not know how to measure sorrow. People worry about me because I had cancer, but, somehow, I think every age and every situation has its equivalent pain. I am not sure cancer is the worst thing I have gone or will go through. Leukemia was a straightforward enemy. I never had any compassion for it. Only determination to lick it. My feelings for Custer are huge and conflicted. And I wonder if I should have tested my equipment on someone I like a lot less. But what can I do if I am not interested in anyone else?

The other men my age are too stupid.

And Custer is my favorite human.

I continued to walk and think about these unquantifiables until it started to drizzle, then splotch, then big muddy puddles formed on the aqueduct.

I know Custer's grief weighs as much as mine, but I wonder if we will be able to console each other. I do not know why two people who care about each other are sometimes the last people to give each other solace. As it is, we glide by one another, with full knowledge of our cargo. Yet we say nothing.

As I stared at the aqueduct, the words Maria once taught me played inside my head. I think Samuel Beckett said them. And they go like this: "The tears of the world are in constant quantity. For each one who begins to weep, somewhere else another stops."

For a moment on that mucky road, the puddles—brimming, spilling, and spreading with water—seemed to me nothing more than nature's tear vials. And when the clouds raced by, I knew the rain had to fall somewhere else.